I0641295

Fire Chief

Firehouse Blues Series: Book 7

AE Moran

The Invisible Publishing Company

Firehouse Blues Series

Contents

Chapter 1: Naomi

I glance up at the firehouse roster on the bulletin board and cast a desperate look around at my crewmates.

Ellis Barrett sits off to one side and doesn't get involved in our conversation. He won't even look at us.

"What are we going to do?" I ask.

"There's nothing we can do," Chris Daniels replies. "We just have to keep working with the few people we have left. We have to keep responding to calls whenever people need us even if we respond with less than a full crew."

I hate to look back at the roster, but I have to. "We only have three more days left on the roster. One of us should step in and decide who is going to work on which shifts."

"Who do you recommend for that job?" Brooke Elsworth asks. "John could barely fill the roster as it was when he was alive. Now Andy is gone, Leila is on indefinite maternity leave, and Keith, Danny, and Emily are out of the picture. We're missing two paramedics, two of our most senior firefighters, and an EMT."

"I think Carter should do it," Billy Cates jerks his thumb at Carter Holt. He stands to one side with Sophie McNish.

"Don't look at me!" Carter exclaims. "Chief Brewer and I together couldn't fill that roster at the best of times. The rest of us don't have a prayer now."

"Then what are we supposed to do instead?" Josh Abbott asks. "Monday is going to roll around and none of us will know where to work or when."

"You worked on the roster before, Carter," Jessie Nash points out. "You're the only person here who is qualified even to look at it and decide."

Carter puffs out his cheeks. "I will if you really want me to. I can't promise I'll be able to do a good job."

"Anything will be better than nothing," Brooke tells him.

"You can roster us on partial shifts and spread us thinner than usual," Sophie suggests. "Why don't you cut either the ladder truck crew or one of the ambulances? Then you'll have enough people to crew three vehicles instead of four."

"That's against the state regulations," Carter points out. "We could get slapped with an injunction to stop all services if we did that."

"Well, what the hell are we supposed to do?!" Billy demands. "If we stop services or we don't show up, people are going to start dying out there."

"I don't make the state laws, man!" Carter counters. "I just work here."

"You're a supervisor for the State Health and Safety Commission," Josh points out. "Who else are we supposed to turn to?"

"If I'm acting in my capacity as a supervisor for the State Health and Safety Commission, then I would have no choice but to tell you to close the firehouse right now," Carter fires back.

"Forget that!" Jessie snaps. "Never in a million years."

"I know," Carter replies. "That's exactly what I'm saying."

"It sounds to me like we need to take the whole State Health and Safety Commission out of the picture," I chime in. "No offense to you, Carter, but we need to completely ignore regulations on this and just do what we have to do."

"That's why I can't be involved in organizing the roster," Carter points out. "You need to get someone else."

"Like who?" Caleb Watts asks.

Almost as if his words made it happen, we hear a car door slam outside. We all turn around and stare in shocked silence when Keith and Danny Brewer walk into the garage with their wives, Leila and Emily.

No one says anything until the family stops in front of the bulletin board.

Keith glares at everyone in outright hatred. I've never seen him so furious. Danny's eyes are still raging bloodshot. He probably hasn't stopped crying since his brother died.

I really don't blame him. John Brewer was a hero to us all. He couldn't have died in a more tragic and heartless way—and we all had to witness it.

Leila and Emily aren't doing so well, either, but at least they're here—and they all show up in their uniforms.

Billy breaks the awkward silence. "What's going on, man? Are you all okay? We were worried when we didn't hear from you."

"We're fine," Keith clips in his most brutal undertone. His voice, manner, and the appearance of all four of them say the opposite. "What's going on with all of you?"

"We were just trying to figure out what to do about next week's roster," I tell him. "None of us can decide what to do. We've been so shorthanded without you four—and Andy of course."

"None of us can decide who's making the decisions about anything around here," Brooke adds. "We need to order oxygen tanks and other supplies and none of us knows how to operate the system or who to contact."

"I'll handle that." Keith shoves past us to the board, unpins the old roster, takes it down, and frowns at it.

"What do you mean—you'll handle it?" Caleb asks. "What will you handle and how will you handle it?"

"I'll handle everything—the roster, the ordering, everything." Keith looks up and casts a hard glare around the circle of faces. "I'm the most senior firefighter and the highest-ranked member of the department. I'll act as Fire Chief until the State Commission appoints someone else."

"You?!" Billy gasps. *"You'll* act as Fire Chief?"

"Did you want to take the job instead?" Keith looks around at us a second time. "Does any of you want to put your hand up for the job?"

No one says a word, not even Carter. I don't know if he is qualified to act as Fire Chief. This stuff is way above my pay grade.

Keith only nods and waves the old roster at us. "All of you come upstairs and we'll work this out right now." He calls across the garage. "You come, too, Ellis. You're part of this."

Keith heads for the stairs. The rest of us gape at each other with our mouths open while Danny, Leila, and Emily follow him up to John's office.

The rest of us file upstairs behind them. Ellis comes last. He hangs back and leaves a huge gap between us and him.

He's been acting like this since John's death. Ellis hasn't been the same since. I'm surprised he keeps showing up for work at all.

We jam ourselves into John's office. The place doesn't look the same without him.

No one has touched anything since he left it last. All his paperwork, computers, and stationery still sit in the same places.

All his certifications cover the walls. No one has come in here to take them down.

Keith slots behind the desk, wakes up the computer, and sits down in the chair to navigate around.

The rest of us watch in shocked silence. I guess I can't be surprised that Keith is taking over as acting Fire Chief, now that John is gone. I wouldn't trust anyone else to do the job.

I wouldn't want anyone else to do the job. Anyone else doing the job would seem like an insult to John's memory.

Keith brings up a document on the screen and switches on an overhead projector. It casts an image of the document onto the wall between the bookshelves. We can all see the roster for the last two weeks.

He goes over to it and points at different spots. "So the only shifts we're missing at the moment are Andy's....."

"So...you, Danny, and Emily are coming back to work?" Chris asks. "Are you back....for good?"

Keith nods at her only once. "That was the plan. We didn't plan to quit permanently and the crew needs us. Leila will return to work to fill Andy's spot...."

"What?!" everyone yells.

"What about Leon?" I ask.

"Leila will bring Leon with her for all her rostered shifts," Keith goes on. "My mom will hang around the firehouse on the shifts when Leila is rostered. Leila will take care of Leon as long as we're in the firehouse making fools of ourselves in the breakroom. When we get a call, Leila will hand off Leon to my mom. She'll take care of him until we get back." He looks around. "Any questions?"

"But what about.....?" Sophie asks and everyone exchanges more nervous glances.

This is the best solution I can think of. It fills all the gaps in the roster ever since Ellen Foreman got hurt and had to quit the crew.

"John was in the middle of interviewing another paramedic to take Leila's place," Keith goes on. "I'll contact the State Commission about whether they want me to continue with the hiring process or if they want us to wait until we get a new Fire Chief. If they tell me to go ahead and this woman really is as promising as John said she was, then we could have another member on our crew before we know it. Then Leila can go back to her maternity leave and we'll all go back to work."

His words set the Fates in motion again. The fire alarm goes off right then.

We all crowd out of the office and back to the garage. Keith gets behind the wheel of the rescue truck with Billy next to him just like old times.

I exchange glances with Jessie when we get into the back seat. Carter, Caleb, and Danny take the middle seat.

They don't joke around the way they used to. Keith puts the truck into gear and we pull out onto the street heading for the call address.

Chapter 2: Naomi

"What do we got?!" Keith yells over the sirens on our way across town.

Billy checks the dispatch notes on the truck's onboard computer. "House fire in one of the outer neighborhoods—no, two house fires! A gas main ruptured in one of them and the flow backed up to the house next door. Both families still trapped inside and unaccounted for!"

None of us say anything after that apart from Billy giving Keith directions. Jessie and I get busy swapping out the medical gear in the jump kit for fire and trauma equipment.

The guys pull on their SCBAs and check their masks and regulators just in case. We're all extra careful to check our equipment after Andy Skinner tried to kill Carter by tampering with his mask.

We get to the scene all too soon. The Police are already there. "The gas is turned off to the whole neighborhood!" one of the officers tells us.

"Any sign of the families?" Keith asks.

The officer shakes his head. "Nothing. They were all inside when it happened."

We turn our attention to the two houses. Flames almost completely consume both of them.

"The gas went off in the kitchens," the officer tells us. "You should be able to get in through the garages. I can't promise you'll find anything, but you can try it."

Keith starts barking orders at everyone to get out the hoses and spray down the flames. He divides us into teams with me, Jessie, Caleb, and Ellis assigned to one house. Chris, Josh, Danny, and Billy take the other house.

"If anything goes wrong or it's too dangerous, pull the plug and get the hell out of there!" Keith orders. "Don't take any chances. If you don't see anyone, get out."

Caleb nods and the four of us pull on our masks. Caleb and Ellis enter the garage first.

It's all clear until Caleb pushes open the door leading into the house. Fire billows through the interior hallway.

We crawl inside on our hands and knees. The floor is the only place cool enough for us to survive. We make it as far as the dining room and spot five members of the family sprawled across the floor.

Their chairs lie on their sides with the wall adjoining the kitchen completely blasted out.

Scorching flames plume into the dining room. The explosion has thrown everyone across the room. They would be dead by now if they were lying any closer to the fire.

We charge into the room and start dragging everyone into the hall. Caleb throws the two younger children over his shoulders, but he still can't stand upright. "Get everyone out on the double!" he yells.

Ellis takes hold of the father by the shoulders of his suit jacket. I grab the mother by her wrists and start towing her toward the door.

Jessie grabs the two older children by their collars. The four of us start across the floor heading back to the hall, but the fire escalates faster than any of us realizes.

Caleb gets to the hall first and has to draw back when a monstrous coil of flame rolls through the doorway. It forces him to retreat. "We can't get out that way!"

He rushes past us toward the dining room windows, but before any of us can move, another explosion goes off somewhere.

It throws all of us to the ground and Caleb topples. The two kids go flying as another plume of fire consumes the wall with the windows in it. The heat makes all of us cower.

I cover the mother with my body to protect her and cast a helpless look around.

Caleb isn't moving. I crawl over to him. He's breathing and he has a pulse, but he's unconscious.

Ellis pulls himself across the floor wincing and hissing through his teeth behind his mask. He tugs the father one painstaking inch at a time to safety, but I would have to be blind not to see that Ellis is hurt, too.

Jessie and I exchange glances. I straighten up to go get Caleb's axe. My one thought is to hack my way through the wall back into the garage. I just hope to God the fire hasn't gotten that far.

No one outside knows where we are. No one even knows we're in trouble.

Before I can make my move, something strikes the wall to my left. I glance that way and stare in amazement as the head of an axe chops through from outside.

The axe yanks free and strikes again and again. It breaks down the wall and I blink up at a firefighter I've never met. He wears turnouts, a helmet, and an SCBA just like ours, but he doesn't belong to our crew.

He's an older guy with salt-and-pepper grey hair and a lined face, but he's as big as Keith if not bigger. This stranger might even be as big as Billy.

The guy breaks a hole in the wall between us and the garage, tears out the broken boards, and thrusts his arms through. "Hand me the kids first!" he yells.

Jessie and I jump up even though the dining room is still dangerous. I grab one of the kids who has fallen off of Caleb's shoulder, carry the kid over to the hole, and hand the child to this strange firefighter.

I don't care who the guy is as long as we get ourselves and these people out alive.

The guy takes the kid and hands the child to Leila who stands behind him. I catch a glimpse of a line of people passing the kid all the way back to the ambulance.

Jessie shows up next and hands out the second child. Then I bring over the third one. That leaves the two parents, Caleb, and Ellis.

Jessie starts dragging the mother toward the hole. I drag the father, but Jessie can't lift the mother by herself.

I have to break off and help her. Then she helps me lift the father. It takes both of us working together to wedge the unconscious patients out of the building.

Ellis hobbles over to the opening by himself. Jessie helps him while I go back to get Caleb.

He's too big for me to lift, so I have to drag him, too. I growl and then bellow from the effort when I see the fire chewing closer to us. Why does he have to weigh so much?

In a heartbeat, the strange firefighter appears at my side. "I'll take him!" the guy yells. "Get out of here before the whole thing collapses!"

Collapses? The fire must be a lot worse than we realized. I turn around and see that I'm the only member of our crew left in the house besides Caleb.

I wait just long enough to see the stranger sling Caleb over his shoulder. This unknown firefighter can carry Caleb easily even though the guy is so much older than the rest of us.

I turn away to make a break for it, but as soon as I turn my back on the guy, another blast of fire pelts through a different wall and flattens me.

I swim in and out of consciousness for a second before I feel the stranger pick me up in his arms. My vision comes into focus just long enough to look up at his face.

He carries me like a baby instead of in a fire carry. He gazes down at me through his mask. He's really handsome for a guy his age. He has deep black eyes and finely etched features that make him look distinguished and charismatic.

He carries me to the hole he chopped in the wall and turns me sideways to pass me through it. Right then, another brutal concussion strikes the house and knocks me out.

Chapter 3: Naomi

I struggle back to consciousness and try to sit up. Someone shines a light in my eyes. "Take it easy, girl," someone tells me. "Don't move around so fast."

I groan when I recognize Josh bending over me. I'm in the Emergency Department of Howe County Hospital.

"What happened?" I croak. "Some strange guy got me out of the house."

"He saved all of you." Josh palpates my neck. "Do you have any pain here?"

"No, I'm fine." I look up and then look around the room. "Where is he? *Who* is he?"

"We don't know. He got knocked down by the same blast that hit you. He's upstairs getting a CT scan on his head."

"So....you never found out who he is? Where did he come from?"

"We don't know." Josh puts his pen light away and goes on giving me a physical examination. "He showed up in the middle of the call and went into the garage. We were all too busy dealing with the fire and other patients. By the time anyone realized you were in trouble, he was already in there pulling you and your patients out."

I groan and rub my eyes again. "Are Ellis and Caleb all right?"

"They're fine. Caleb got a concussion. Ellis pulled a ligament in his thigh. They're both back at the firehouse already. You and the mystery man are the only ones still here."

He straightens up and picks up his clipboard to finish filling out his paperwork. "If your vision is tracking right, you can leave, too. Drew and I are going back in the ambulance in a minute. You can ride with us "

I help Josh and Drew restock the ambulance while Josh gives me the rundown on the rest of the patients. They're all upstairs in the burn unit getting treated for smoke inhalation, but they're all going to be fine, too, thanks to our mystery man.

"I really can't handle any more mystery men coming into my life," Drew teases when we load into the ambulance. "One was enough."

Josh grins at him. "We might never find out who this guy is. He might have just been passing through town and happened to see what was happening."

We talk about the mystery guy on the way back to the firehouse. "He wasn't young, either," I point out. "He couldn't have been less than forty."

"A guy that old shouldn't be doing frontline field work anymore," Drew remarks. "He should be sitting behind a desk."

"Be glad he is doing frontline field work," Josh counters. "Four of our crew and five patients are alive right now because he had the balls to step in."

"He didn't just have the balls," I add. "He was incredibly strong. He picked up Caleb and carried him with no problem. The guy was a beast."

Drew pulls into the garage. The rest of the crew works to restock their vehicles—all except Caleb and Ellis.

Caleb stands off to one side talking to Keith. Ellis sits in a corner staring at the wall like he usually does. Not even Jessie dares to go near him.

Danny helps restock the rescue truck. The crew tiptoes around him and I spot a bunch of people studying him on the side. I wish I could do something to make this easier for him.

Emily is here, so Danny already has everything and everyone he needs. He has Ellen, Keith, and Leila to support him—and nothing will make it better anyway.

Maybe just getting back to work will soften the blow in time. I can only hope.

Keith finishes talking to Caleb and comes over to me and Jessie. "I need to take statements from both of you for the incident report. I can't get anything out of Caleb or Ellis, so I need to rely on you two." He gives both of us a hard look. "Is it true that some unknown civilian stepped in and pulled you all out?"

"I don't think he was a civilian," I reply. "He was wearing turnouts and an SCBA and he knew exactly what he was doing. I would be very surprised if he wasn't a trained firefighter."

"You don't know where he came from, do you?" Keith asks. "Or his name?"

"I didn't see him until he started hacking his way through the wall. We were both trapped inside until then."

He turns to me. "You were inside with him the longest. Did he tell you his name?"

"He didn't have time to and we didn't ask. He opened the wall and started barking orders.....kind of like you do—and John did. He just took charge of the whole scene like he owned the place."

Keith blows out a breath and bends over his tablet. "It's the craziest thing I've ever seen."

"You don't know who the guy was?" Jessie asks. "The hospital didn't say anything?"

"I didn't get a chance to ask, either. I was too busy dealing with Caleb, Ellis, and the rest of the crew."

"So....do you want us to get back to work now?" I ask and take a chance to peer closer at him. "If you need any help from us—or anything else—you just have to say so. We're all here for you—for your whole family. You know that, right?"

He barely looks at me. He mumbles, "Thanks."

I expect him to walk away, but right then, three different men walk into the garage.

One of them is Police Chief Jim Walker. He always worked closely with John Brewer.

I don't know the other two men. Chief Walker wears his Police uniform. The other two men wear business suits.

The three of them come toward us, but Carter cuts them off and shakes hands with one of the men in a suit.

They stand there talking and shooting glances past Carter's shoulder at Keith standing there.

Carter nods and escorts the three men over to us. Chief Walker shakes hands with Keith. "How you doing, Keith?" Chief Walker asks.

Keith shrugs and looks away. "About like you'd expect. How you doing?"

"I'm making it. This is Salvatore Guzman of the Howe City Council and this is Emerson Freeman of the State Health and Safety Commission."

Keith dips his chin once. His expression doesn't soften in the slightest. "What can I do for you gentlemen?"

"We want you to be the first to know that we've appointed a new Fire Chief for Howe Firehouse," Emerson Freeman announces. "His name is Duke Broebeck. He has experience managing six other fire-houses. He's very professional and he'll take good care of your people."

Keith compresses his lips and growls through gritted teeth. "Good. We need a new Chief."

"We understand he intervened in one of your calls today," Chief Walker interjects. "He happened to be driving past and saw some of your crew in trouble. He's downtown in the hospital right now."

Keith's head shoots up and Jessie and I both gasp. "That guy....is our new Fire Chief?!" Jessie blurts out.

The three men look at me and Jessie. "You met him?" Emerson Freeman asks.

"He saved our lives!" I blurt out. "He got all of us out of a burning house. We didn't know who he was!"

"I can't make any better recommendation than that," Chief Walker replies. "He starts on Monday. I'm sure your crew will make him welcome and give him the same dedicated service you gave John."

The three men shake hands with Keith and Carter and then leave.

"That's amazing!" Jessie breathes after they disappear. "Another caped crusader comes out of the woodwork to save the day."

I glance up at Keith, but he only storms off to the stairs and barges upstairs. He doesn't come back.

Chapter 4: Duke

I get out of my truck in the parking lot behind Howe Firehouse.

Emerson Freeman of the State Health and Safety Commission meets me there and grins when he shakes hands. "Ready for your first day of work?"

"Piece of cake. I do this shit every day."

He gets serious. "Not like this. This crew....they're different."

"What do you mean? They have more decorations between them than every other crew I've worked with combined."

"I don't mean their job performance. They're all very dedicated."

"Then what's the problem?"

"They're.....they're a family. They're extremely close-knit—and they just lost their last Fire Chief in a tragic accident."

"I know. I don't see what that has to do with me."

He raises both hands. "Just hear me out, man. The senior firefighter on the crew is the former Chief's brother. He's really broken up about his brother's death."

"Oh, yeah. I remember." I flip open the files the Commission gave me on this job posting. "Keith Brewer, isn't it? His younger brother Danny works here, too, doesn't he?"

"Keith has been really touchy about his brother's death—as you can imagine. The whole crew is a mess, but he's the worst. You'll see when you meet him."

"The paperwork says he's been acting as Fire Chief since his brother's death. Is he going to have a problem with someone else taking over? If he's already doing the job, maybe he should keep doing it."

"We already tried to offer it to him, but he turned us down. He says he doesn't want to take his brother's place. When we told him you were taking over, he said it was a good thing because Howe needs a real Fire Chief."

I frown. "That's odd. He should have been happy to get a promotion."

"You don't understand, man. His brother's death....."

I frown at him. "What happened? The paperwork doesn't say anything about it."

"It's complicated. I'm sure you'll find out the whole story soon enough. Just....don't be too hard on them if they offer resistance. This crew has been through a lot—and they're worth it. If you can win their respect, they'll give you everything. That's what John Brewer did. He brought them together and made them what they are. It's going to take a big man to fill his shoes."

"All right. Thanks for the warning."

He waves over his shoulder. "Come on inside and I'll introduce you—properly this time."

I grab my duffel bag out of the truck and follow him into the garage. The crew is all busy working on their trucks the way they should be at this time of the morning.

They all stop what they're doing and dead silence falls over the garage when I walk in. I recognize a bunch of people from the call the other day and they obviously recognize me.

I do the quickest possible assessment of the people in front of me. I've reviewed their personnel files as well as I can.

Now I go through them and connect up the names and pictures in their files to the real people.

Keith Brewer is a husky, grizzled, bearded biker-type. He glares at me in stony fury. Now I understand what Emerson meant.

His brother Danny is younger and much better looking. His picture in his file shows him smiling. Now he looks like someone has sucked all the life out of him.

He stares out at the world through bloodshot eyes. Dark bags hang under his shadowy eye sockets like he hasn't slept in a few weeks.

Carter Holt has been badly burned over his whole head, face, neck, and arms. He looks like something out of my worst nightmares, but he's as sturdy and powerfully built and regards me as directly as any of the others.

Ellis Barrett hangs back behind the rest of the crew and barely looks at anyone. His file lists numerous incidents of practical jokes he's played on his crewmates.

Now he looks like he can barely summon the enthusiasm to come to work at all. He makes only the barest showing of joining the group and he obviously only does that much because he can't ignore me entirely.

The others all regard me with a healthy dose of suspicion. Tears well up in Leila Cunningham's eyes the minute she sees me. She starts dabbing her eyes with a tissue to dry them.

I recognize the two paramedics from that first call I attended. Naomi McFee is a short, dark-haired witchy little fox with penetrating, haunted eyes that send a tendril of fire through my guts.

She studies me much more seriously than the others. I don't see any outright hostility from her. She mostly just looks insatiably curious—and passionate.

Her eyes blaze with something like demonic fire. She looks up at me with the same expression she used on me during the fire. I have a hard time looking away.

The other paramedic is another petite woman with soft, hay-blonde hair and green eyes. Jessie Nash is quite pretty, too, but she doesn't give off the sense of dark fire that Naomi does.

"I'd like to introduce you all to Duke Broebeck, Howe County Fire Department's new Fire Chief," Emerson announces. "He comes highly qualified and I know all of you will give him your best service. Duke will take over for Keith and Keith will return to his normally rostered duties as of today."

No one says anything for a second. That silence stretches longer and longer and longer.

I don't know what to say. I could give the usual speech about how happy I am to be here and how much I'm looking forward to working with such a decorated crew.

I could tell them that I hope we all become a family the way they were with John Brewer, but I don't say that.

None of those things seem to fit this situation. I've taken over for other Fire Chiefs killed in the line of duty. I've never taken over a crew like this before.

They all just stand there staring at me like they can't figure out what to say, either.

Without warning, Keith Brewer breaks out of line, storms off to the garage door, and walks out of the building without a backward glance.

Everyone stares after him and then all eyes shoot back to me. Am I supposed to go after him—or fire him—or do anything about that?

Emerson gets my attention by shuffling his feet just then.

"You can go," I tell him. "I'll take over from here."

He gives me a questioning look as if to ask if I'm sure I want him to leave me alone with these dangerous people.

They aren't dangerous. They're emotional about losing their former Chief. They really must have cared about him.

I can understand Keith and Danny reacting this way after losing their brother—and now Keith having to take over his brother's job. That has to be hard on anyone.

Now Keith has to stand by and watch someone else take over his brother's job. I'm beginning to understand what Emerson means about this crew.

I nod toward the door. "Go," I murmur.

He glances around. The rest of the crew stands there in silence. This is rapidly turning into one of the most uncomfortable experiences of my career.

He finally walks out and disappears out of my life—for the moment at least. That leaves me alone with the crew, but I have no plans to stand here waiting for someone to come up with something to say.

I also have no plans to give a meaningless speech. These people might not want me here, but I'm here to do a job, not to make friends with them.

I walk away to the stairs leading up to the Fire Chief's office.

I walk in and see John Brewer's certifications framed on the wall. No one has taken them down. I'll have to do that so I can make this office my own.

Now isn't the time, though. The crew would probably lynch me if I took down John Brewer's certifications now. I'll have to wait until emotions cool off.

I sit down behind the desk and wake up the computer. It opens into a document listing the crew roster for the next two weeks.

I see a bunch of problems with it right away—including that Leila Cunningham plans to work with her baby boy in tow. That is never going to happen on my watch.

I rewrite the roster and wrangle a bunch of different people to cover Leila's shifts. It isn't easy. I have to give a few other paramedics overtime.

She isn't slated to complete her maternity leave in five months. I can afford a little overtime until she decides to come back—or I hire some new people to fill the gaps.

My curiosity is getting the better of me. I need to know more about the people under me, so I pull up the records on John Brewer's death.

It takes me a while to rummage through both the personnel files of the last six months and then to access the Police database before I get to the truth.

For some reason known only to himself, former paramedic Andrew Skinner developed an instant dislike for Carter Holt.

Maybe Andy got a bee under his bonnet because he didn't want an outsider conducting a Health and Safety audit on Howe Firehouse.

The records don't indicate that, though.

The first incident happened when Carter was attending a call and ordered Andy to bring him restraint straps to subdue a combative patient. Andy ignored the order.

Carter then used his authority with John Brewer to get the Fire Chief to formally reprimand Andy. Good for Carter. Brewer should have disciplined an insubordinate employee like that a long time ago.

I can't fathom why a professionally trained paramedic would ignore a valid order from his superior officer—unless Andy had an issue with the way Carter looks.

The incident sent Andy into a downward spiral of irrationality bordering on the insane. He accused Carter of coming between Andy and Sophie McNish—who had already broken up with him years earlier.

Andy used the incident to try to get back together with her. When she turned him down, he blamed Carter even though there was nothing going on between her and Carter at the time.

Andy escalated things by sabotaging Carter's SCBA so his mask and regulator failed in the middle of a dangerous call. It would have killed Carter, especially since he was in the process of saving Andy's life during the same call.

They both survived, and when Andy got charged with attempted murder, he fought the charge so he could get himself released on bail pending the outcome.

He waited until the crew was having a friendly social barbecue at the beach, showed up with a gun, and tried to shoot Carter. Ellis Barrett tackled Carter out of the way in time to save his life and the shot hit John Brewer instead.

Now Andy is in prison upstate. He was incarcerated without bond immediately after the shooting. He hasn't been released since.

He pled guilty to second-degree manslaughter and two counts of attempted murder against Carter. Now Andy is just awaiting his sentencing hearing.

I lean back in my chair taking it all in. Wow. That is one hell of a story.

This explains everything I'm seeing downstairs. It explains why Ellis is so standoffish, why Keith is so hostile, and why Danny is so emotionally destroyed by this incident.

It really is amazing that any of the crew is still working at all. They must be incredibly dedicated to keep the firehouse open and operational despite this disaster.

This makes me admire Keith Brewer even more. He's going through the worst pain of his life, but he still sacked it up, stepped into his brother's place, and ran this place.

He could have kept on running it. He could have become Fire Chief. Then I would never have set foot in this place.

I understand now why he doesn't want it. He doesn't want to dishonor his brother's memory.

Taking over for John must have been the hardest thing Keith Brewer ever had to do. He must have been counting down the minutes before someone else came in and took the place off his hands.

Chapter 5: Naomi

The crew glances around at each other after Duke Broebeck disappears upstairs on his way to John Brewer's office.

"Now what are we supposed to do?" Jessie half-whispers.

"I guess we just get back to work," Caleb remarks. "We go back to doing what we were doing before—what we would be doing if John was still here."

"How can we?" Brooke quavers. "How can we keep working when some stranger is sitting upstairs in John's office?"

"It isn't John's office anymore," I remark. "It's Duke's office now."

"How can you say that when John's awards and certifications are still all over the walls?!" Vince Jaeger asks.

"Do you want to be the one to go up there and take down John's certifications?" I ask. "I don't."

"It will always be John's office," Billy mutters. "I don't care who the new Fire Chief is."

Sophie glances toward the garage door. "What are we going to do about Keith? He could get fired for walking out in the middle of a shift."

"We don't do anything about Keith," Josh replies. "He's a big boy. He can handle his own business."

"If Duke is half the man I think he is, he'll understand why Keith, Danny, and the rest of the Brewers have a problem with this," I point out. "The State Commission must have told Duke what happened."

Caleb spins around to confront me. "Why are you defending him?! He can't just walk in here and start taking over!"

"Leave her alone," Chris interjects. "Duke saved her and Jessie from that fire. He must be a good guy."

"Duke saved *you* from that fire, too, Caleb," I point out. "Cut the guy some slack. He's just doing his job—which is to walk in here and start taking over and giving us all orders. What did you think was going to happen? Keith couldn't be our Fire Chief forever."

"Why not?" Caleb demands. "He knows us all and he's perfectly well qualified."

"The State Commission would have had to advertise that job publicly before they hired someone to fill John's position," Carter points out. "Keith could have applied for it."

"Then the Commission is screwed up for not hiring him," Caleb fires back. "You can't expect him to just sit back and accept it when they passed him up."

"What makes you think they passed him up?" Josh asks. "We don't even know if he applied for it."

Just then, Keith walks back into the firehouse. He doesn't come toward us. He heads for the rescue truck to go on with his checks—which is what the rest of us should be doing instead of minding other people's business.

"Keith!" Caleb calls out.

Keith diverts to face us, but his expression never clears. He never lets down his guard to show how much he's hurting inside.

"Did the State Commission tell you why they turned you down for the Fire Chief job?" Caleb asks. "It's messed up that you didn't get it."

"They didn't turn me down," Keith replies. "I turned them down."

"You what?!" Jessie gasps.

"They offered it to me first—before they advertised it to anyone else. I told them I didn't want it." He makes a face. "You couldn't pay me to do that job."

"You mean.....?" Caleb trails off.

"So Duke...." Sophie begins.

"What's your problem with Duke?" Keith snaps. "He's here to do a job. Get used to it. We were bound to get a new Fire Chief eventually. Now he's here. You know he's a good guy. Just do your jobs." He claps his hands. "Get to it. Come on. Quit stalling."

We wander back to the trucks and get back to work. Jessie and I climb into the back and start checking the drug box.

Josh and Carter get into the middle seat and start going over the SCBAs with a fine-toothed comb. Carter has a thing about SCBAs ever since his mask failed.

Keith and Billy get into the front and run the early-morning test transmissions on the radio system with dispatch.

"Are you and Sophie still planning to have your wedding at the firehouse?" Jessie asks Carter.

"We haven't decided if we should or not," he replies without looking up from his pressure valve. "We were waiting until the Brewers came back on duty so we could ask them how they feel."

"Go ahead and have it," Keith replies over his shoulder. "Why wait?"

"We didn't want to offend anyone," Carter replies. "I'll tell Sophie you're okay with it."

"It isn't like we own the place," Keith mutters. "Do whatever you want to do."

"What about the barbecues?" Josh asks. "We were scheduled to have a barbecue this weekend. John started the barbecues and pool nights and everything. Are we still doing them?"

Keith spins around and scowls over the seat. "Who said anything about stopping the barbecues? We aren't stopping them just because John is gone."

"No one has organized it," Jessie points out. "No one on the crew even knows if it's going ahead or not."

Keith turns the rest of the way around and glares at all of us. "No one has told you?! Are you serious?"

Jessie and I exchange glances. "How could they? Who would organize it?"

"Ellen and Leila are organizing it!" Keith snaps. "Are you telling me they haven't told anyone?"

Josh and Carter both glance at us. "No. No one said anything about it."

Keith compresses his lips and turns back to checking the dashboard lights. "That's just great," he mutters. "I'm going to have to bust some heads."

"So....it's on?" Jessie asks.

"Of course it's on!" he barks. "They have all the drinks and ice and everything in my freezer at home. I can't believe they didn't tell you."

"Oh. Okay." I brighten up. "Hey! We should invite Duke—just to let him know he's welcome."

"Good idea," Keith snarls over his shoulder.

"You should invite him, Naomi," Jessie tells me. "You know him the best."

"ME?!" I practically shriek. "I don't know him at all!"

"You were with him in the burning house," Josh points out.

"That doesn't mean I got to know him!" I counter. "We exchanged less than a dozen words. We were too busy saving patients."

"That's a dozen words more than the rest of us have exchanged with him," Carter adds. "Just invite him. How hard can it be?"

"But.....I can't just waltz into his office and invite him to the barbecue! No way!"

"You were the one who said to cut him some slack because he was just doing his job," Billy reminds me. "Cut the guy some slack and invite him to the barbecue."

"But why me?!" I demand. "Why do I have to be the one?"

"Who else is going to do it?" Jessie asks.

"You!" I tell her and then turn to the others. "Or you or you or you. I don't want to go up there!"

"Come on, sweetie," Keith tells me. "Take one for the team."

"NO!" I holler.

Billy shoots me a grin over the seat. "What's wrong? You aren't scared of big, bad Duke, are you?"

"I'm not scared of him...."

"You are so," Josh teases. "What's the matter? What can possibly go wrong?"

I shut my mouth in a hurry. I don't want to think about what could possibly go wrong from me walking into Duke's office and inviting him to the barbecue.

I might fall flat on my face....or make an idiot of myself.....or he might get the wrong idea about why I'm there at all. A lot can go wrong and probably will.

I have a flashback to one of the last things John ever said to us as a crew. He told us to give new people a chance and to welcome them as a part of the family.

If they don't work out, that's on them. We won't know if someone could be part of the family if we didn't welcome them and give them a chance first.

I'm one of the few people on the crew besides Keith who has been speaking up for Duke from the beginning.

I seem to be the only person who realizes that he actually could be a good Fire Chief. Why shouldn't he be? He must be very experienced. The State Commission wouldn't have hired him if he wasn't.

So why am I so anxious about going to talk to him?

The rest of the crew goes on with their work. They don't notice how flustered I am or else they pretend not to notice.

I get another flashback of gazing up at Duke's face during the fire. He gazed down at my face with.....

I don't know what kind of expression it was. He's amazingly good-looking and magnetically charismatic in every way.

He's also a lot older than I am and now he's my boss. It isn't like anything could happen between us.

I don't even want something to happen to us.

I can't forget the way he looked at me during the fire—or maybe it was the way I was looking at him.

I keep drifting back into the memory of him carrying me out of the dining room. I've never felt that sense of safety and relief with anyone—like nothing bad could ever happen to me as long as I was in his arms.

His eyes and face gave me that feeling, too. I get a rush of the same overwhelming happiness and rightness just thinking about looking up at him like that.

I shake that out of my head. I can't think like that. I have a job to do here and so does he. We aren't going there.

Now I have to invite him to the barbecue. I didn't mean to volunteer myself by suggesting it. Now I have no choice but to go through with it.

Chapter 6: Duke

I'm just going over the personnel records from the firehouse staff for the dozenth time. I want to find out as much as I can about these people before the shit hits the fan.

A soft knock on my door distracts me. I yell over without looking up. "Come in!"

The door swings open. I freeze in my chair when I see Naomi.

She hesitates before she ventures into the room.

"What's up?" I ask and try to turn it into a joke. "Is the crew getting out the pitchforks yet?"

Her eyes go wide in a look of stark terror. She opens her mouth, but no sound comes out. Okay. That was the wrong thing to say to lighten the mood.

My shoulders slump. I try a different approach. "What's on your mind? Do you want to sit down?"

She gulps hard and looks down at the chair like it might attack her. That probably wasn't the right thing to say, either.

I'm just trying to decide how to break the tense silence when she blurts out, "You know.....we have barbecues.....on the weekends.....every second weekend....at the beach....."

"I know." I frown at her. "Did you come in here to tell me that?"

"We want to invite you....this weekend.....the whole crew does, I mean....not just me....."

She squirms in front of me and I see it all in a flash of insight. She's attracted to me. How charming. She's worried I'll think she came here to ask me out.

I wind up smiling, and before I think to stop myself, I glance down at her body.

She has a petite, trim, curvy figure just as witchy and enticing as the rest of her. Her body seems to radiate the kind of mysterious enchantment I get from her eyes, face, and hair.

She's extremely attractive, but she's also fifteen years younger than I am. She won't be interested in a guy my age—and I'm her boss.

I can't help but smile at her, though. "Thank you for inviting me. I would love to come."

"We just thought....you know.....John started the barbecues.....so we weren't sure if we should keep doing them.....and just now....Keith told us Ellen and Leila were organizing it......and John said....." She breaks off, clamps her eyes and lips shut, and shakes her head. "Sorry. I'm rambling."

I sit back in my chair and watch her. This is absolutely beyond sweet. She's getting all flustered trying to talk to me—not because she's scared of me, but because she finds me attractive.

This is a fine way to start my first day as Fire Chief in this department, but it sure is nice that someone appreciates me. I've never been more flattered.

I decide to make it easier for her by changing the subject. "I'm sorry for what I said about the crew getting out the pitchforks. Maybe you could tell me how everyone is feeling about a new Fire Chief stepping into John's place."

She looks away, but those magical eyes always wind up coming back to meet mine.

I get a flashback of the way she looked at me during the fire—almost like she was intoxicated by sex and looking up at me in the throes of passion.

A lick of adrenaline burns my guts when I think that, but I can never act on it. I'll just have to admire her from afar and envy the lucky guy who finally gets his hands on her.

She probably already has a boyfriend or even a fiancé. She's a treasure.

"Well...you know...." she stammers. "No one is happy about it .....but then again...no one is happy about anything where John is concerned.....and you know how Keith and Danny are.....they're never going to get over this...."

"So Keith and Danny are upset about it? I understand."

"Not with you!" she blurts out. "They have nothing against you. Keith is down there defending you more than anyone."

I raise my eyebrows. "He is?"

"Absolutely!" She starts talking way too fast and way too loud. "He's telling everyone to give you a chance.....and that you're a good guy and everything....."

She trails off and looks around terrified again like she said too much. My heart twists watching her struggle when she realizes she's giving me a compliment.

"I mean....." she blathers. "During the fire....and everything....I just thought....."

So she remembers it, too. I didn't just imagine the way she was looking at me. She felt it then, too.

She finally looks down at her hands. "I'm really grateful for what you did for me....I mean.....I didn't realize you were....."

She breaks off again, shuffles her feet for a minute, and bolts from the room. She leaves the door open and I hear her footsteps racing down the stairs.

I chuckle to myself, but those words change things for me.

She is so unbelievably beautiful—in every way. That's nothing compared to the way she looked when I carried her out of the burning house.

I turn back to my computer to continue work, but I can't stop thinking about her.

It would be amazing to see her like that—all wide-eyed and awestruck in the throes of sex. It would be wonderful to see her looking up at me with that kind of passionate rapture and to know that she feels that way about me.

It would be wonderful to feel that from any woman.

Now she's right here in front of me—and that memory is right here in front of me.

I don't have to wonder what she would look like if I took her like that. I've already seen her like that—and she really was looking up at me like that.

She didn't know who I was then. Now she knows I'm her boss and it could never happen.

It sure is nice to think about, though. That memory is going to keep me warm for a long, long time—probably as long as I keep working here where I have to see her magnificent face every day.

Chapter 7: Naomi

I glance down the beach and shudder in relief when I see that Duke isn't here yet. Maybe he won't come to the barbecue after all. Maybe he'll change his mind or something will come up so he'll have to cancel.

This barbecue is going to be hard enough after John's death. Duke's presence will make it even harder for everyone to relax and get back into the usual routine.

I take a big box of cookies, brownies, potato chips, and other snacks out of the back of my car and hike down to the beach.

Keith and Danny are already down there setting up the barbecue. Leila and Emily set up the picnic table while some of the kids run around on the sand. Only a handful are here now. The rest will come later.

The beach doesn't look right without John here. The three Brewer brothers were always the Guardians of the Barbecue.

I can convince myself that John, Ellen, and Oakleigh just haven't shown up yet. They'll arrive any second now and everything will be fine.

I carry my stuff to the picnic table and hug Leila and Emily. I haven't seen either of them since Duke took over.

One of his first acts as Fire Chief was to take Leila off the roster after Keith put her on it. The rest of the crew is still bristling over this, but Keith defends the decision.

"I only put her on because we needed her," he tells us. "A woman wouldn't be able to bring her baby to work in any other firehouse."

"But we have exactly the same number of staff now that we did before," Brooke points out. "We're short-handed again without Leila filling in."

Keith only shrugs. "That's his decision. Take it up with the boss."

That ends the conversation, but not the grumbling and resentment.

If Andy was here, he would be leading the revolt against Duke's authority. Andy isn't here, so the naysayers are leaderless.

They're also toothless. They don't have the backbone to confront Duke on any decision, especially not one as simple as the crew roster.

That doesn't stop them from muttering behind his back.

I sure wish they would stop. Their constant second-guessing of everything he does is only making life at the firehouse more tense and uncomfortable than it already is.

I help Leila and Emily set up the picnic table and then go back to my car for the second load of munchies. I'm just slamming the trunk when Ellen pulls in with Oakleigh in the back seat.

Ellen smiles at me and waves through the windshield. Oakleigh stares off in a different direction.

Ellen gets out and I hug her. "Hey!" I tell her. "How are you doing?"

She just shrugs and tears come to her eyes. "I'm making it through the day. That's about the best I can do."

I glance toward the car. "How's the baby?"

Ellen lowers her voice to a murmur. "Not good. She's having a hard time." She steers me away. "Let's go. I want to see everyone."

"What about her?" I glance over my shoulder toward the car. Oakleigh doesn't look at me once.

"Just leave her alone. She likes to spend time by herself. She doesn't feel like socializing."

"That's awful!" I exclaim. "The poor thing!"

Ellen struggles to control her lips. "This is so hard for her! First she lost her mother and now her father. I'm all she has left—me and the boys and Leila and Emily and Zeke. The boys have been fantastic with her, but nothing helps."

I want to say more, but nothing will bring John back. That's what Oakleigh really needs and no one can give her that.

I help Ellen carry her supplies down to the picnic table. More of our off-duty crew members show up and they all hug Ellen, too.

Some of the crew remarks about Oakleigh sitting in the back of the car. Ellen has to explain it to everyone. "Just leave her alone," Keith tells everyone. "She'll deal with it in her own way."

We can all see how Keith and Danny are dealing with it. In a little while, Oakleigh gets out of the car and wanders off down the beach by herself.

She doesn't join the other kids' play. Zeke runs around with the others trying to act as normal as possible.

None of the others bother Oakleigh when she sits down on the dunes by herself and stays there.

Ellen makes her a plate of food, hikes out there to give it to her, comes back to join us, and never goes near Oakleigh again.

The fire trucks and ambulances show up with the rest of our rostered crew mates. Ellis is working today. He stands off to one side in his uniform and doesn't get involved in the conversation even when people try to talk to him.

Jessie makes him a plate of food and hands it to him. Other than that, he might as well not be here at all. Would he even come if he wasn't rostered on shift today? I doubt it.

The rest of us start talking the way we always do, but no one jokes around or tells bawdy stories about their more risqué cases and calls.

Everyone keeps it subdued. John Brewer's legacy casts a long shadow over everyone.

None of us would be here if not for him. He was the one who went out of his way to make us into this tightly-knit family.

We wouldn't care about him, his family, or each other if not for his intervention.

We all go through the motions because he would want us to. He would want this bond to survive his death. What else could his life mean if our bond doesn't survive his death?

Ellen and Leila are much more expressive about the situation than Keith or Danny. The two women talk at length about dealing with the fallout from John's death.

Ellen talks about how she has to handle his estate and put his assets in trust for Oakleigh.

"I started work last week," she chokes. "It brought up so many memories of when he used to come into the ED with all of you. I keep waiting for him to come in....but he doesn't."

We all move in to hug her. We've all been going through the same thing waiting for John to come back to the firehouse. He never will—not ever again.

Just then, Jessie whispers, "There he is! He's here!"

A chill rushes up my spine. I don't have to turn around to see who she means.

I plan to pretend Duke isn't here until I absolutely can't avoid it any longer, but the rest of the crew doesn't give me a chance to ignore him.

"You go talk to him, Naomi," Sophie tells me.

"Me?!" I counter. "I'm not going to talk to him! Are you nuts?!"

"You invited him," Josh points out.

"Only because you made me invite him! You go if you want some-one to go."

"I'll go with you," Ellen offers. "Come on, Naomi."

She puts down her drink and limps toward me. Now I have no choice but to go face the firing squad.

I take one glance at Duke and look away. I really have to stop myself from thinking about how attractive he is.

He was so polite and warm when I went to his office. He didn't seem to mind at all when I made an absolute ass of myself.

I knew that was going to happen. Why did I have to get so nervous around him?

I could kick myself for letting him see me rattled. I sure hope he didn't pick up that I find him attractive. That would be disastrous.

Ellen reads my mind. "He looks nice," she murmurs on our way to the parking lot. "He's older than I thought he would be, but he's very nice-looking."

I feel my cheeks burning and look away again. No one has to tell me how nice-looking Duke is.

"Did you find out anything about him?" she asks.

I try to make a joke out of it. "Apart from the fact that he's as much of a stud and a hero as any firefighter on the crew? No, I didn't find out anything about him. He's my boss. It wasn't like I had a chance to interview him before he showed up for his first day of work."

"I just wondered if he told the crew anything about himself."

"The guy from the State Commission said Duke has managed six different firehouses before. He's a pro at this."

"That doesn't tell us anything about his personality, does it?"

I don't really know anything about Duke's personality. I don't need to. I saw enough during the fire.

He's fearless, commanding, confident, and selfless. He's committed to saving lives and he'll stop at nothing to get the job done.

He's also a stickler for the rules. He didn't hesitate to take Leila off the roster and piss off the same crew members who were already against him.

I have to correct myself on that, too. He didn't take her off the roster entirely. He only took her off the roster as long as she was bringing Leon with her.

Duke would be happy to reinstate Leila if she came alone. I know he would. He's too sensible to turn away a perfectly competent paramedic whom we all already know, like, and trust.

I don't try to explain any of this to Ellen. I would probably stick my foot in my mouth again if I tried.

I'll almost certainly stick it in my mouth now when I try to talk to him.

Chapter 8: Naomi

Duke sees us coming and smiles at me when Ellen and I pull up in front of him in the beach parking lot.

"Hi," he greets me.

My cheeks flame again. "Hi," I murmur and wave at Ellen. "This is Ellen Foreman Brewer—John's widow."

She sticks out her hand. "It's a pleasure to meet you. I want to be the first person to welcome you to the family. We're all delighted that you're here."

"Um....thank you." He glances back and forth between us while he shakes her hand.

"I heard about what you did for Naomi and the rest of the crew during that call," she goes on. "I know you'll be the best man to fill John's shoes. You're exactly what this crew needs. I just hope you won't take the stiffness everyone feels now personally. It's just everyone's way of honoring John. It has nothing to do with the respect everyone has for you."

"Thank you," he exclaims. "I understand and I don't take it personally. I'm very sorry for your loss—all of you. I hope my coming to work here doesn't make it harder for you than it already is."

She blinks back tears and compresses her lips to hold them steady. "You aren't. Believe me." She waves behind her. "Please.....come down to the beach and join us. You're very welcome."

Thank the stars Ellen is here to do the talking for me. She even walks between us to protect me from him.

God, what am I doing thinking that way? Duke isn't dangerous.

I'm the one who's a walking catastrophe. I don't know what to say or how to act around him.

He takes a plastic shopping bag out of the bed of his pickup truck. "I brought a few things. I hope you don't mind. I wasn't sure what to bring, so I had to improvise."

He hands Ellen the bag and she opens it to look inside. Her eyes fly open and she gasps and stares at him. "This is great! Thank you so much!"

He smiles at her. "I'm glad you like it."

I glance over to peek into the bag. It's full of sparklers, glowsticks, and other handheld fireworks for the kids.

"Leila is going to be so jealous!" Ellen exclaims. "She never thought of this."

"What do you mean?" he asks.

"Never mind. Come on. People are going to start to think something is wrong if we stay up here any longer."

The three of us head down the beach. The tension becomes palpable when Duke gets near the rest of the group. Conversation dies.

Leila, Sophie, Carter, and a few others come over to talk to him. The rest hang back and either talk to each other or don't talk at all.

I want to run away and bury my head in the sand, but I can't do that when I see just how few people are actually willing to come near the poor guy.

I have to be one of the people that welcomes and supports him. I stay where I am, and when Ellen goes to put his bag on the table, I wind up standing right next to him.

The tension between us spikes off the charts—or maybe I'm the only one who feels it.

He's probably completely oblivious to the fact that I think he's attractive—as if anything could ever happen between us. I'm young enough to be his daughter and he's my boss.

Ellen comes back and the others gather in a second circle while everyone else stays on their side of the barbecue. Keith and Danny are too busy working the grill to get involved.

In a few minutes, Danny leaves to go straighten out some dispute between Zeke and the other kids.

"Naomi was just telling me that you worked in a bunch of other firehouses before this," Ellen tells Duke.

His eyebrows fly up. "She did?" He turns to me. "How did you find out about that?"

My cheeks burn again. "After the fire....." I go through another turbulent confusion of jumbled memories and emotions. "You were in the hospital....and none of us knew who you were....and Jim Walker and Emerson Freeman and someone from the City Council came over to the firehouse to tell Keith that you were going to be our new Fire Chief. Emerson told us that you had a ton of experience....and everything...."

I trail off. Am I even making any sense?

I'm the only member of our crew that heard who conversation besides Keith....oh, and Carter was there, too....and Jessie.

Maybe I shouldn't have heard it. Maybe that was supposed to be private information between Keith and the other three.....so why did they say it in front of me....and in front of Carter and Jessie?

I become aware of Duke staring at me from the side. Does he hate me for spilling information about his work history? Maybe he didn't want anyone at Howe to know about that.

I can't imagine why not. It only proves he's qualified—as if he could get the job without being qualified.

He studies me from the side for way too long. I can't stand here staring off into space while he stares at me.

I wind up looking up at him and almost fall over when I see the look in his eyes.

He immediately looks away and turns to Carter. "I hear you're supervising five Health and Safety officers all over the state. Are you supervising the officer who will be auditing Howe?"

"No, the commission assigned someone else to Howe," Carter replies. "I said I wasn't comfortable even with that level of interest in reviewing an audit on my own firehouse. The Commission was in the middle of redefining the inspectors' coverage ranges anyway, so it worked out."

"Who is our new inspector?" Leila asks.

"He's a young guy named Will Taylor," Carter replies. "He isn't scheduled to audit Howe Firehouse for another five years. I just filed my audit, so Howe doesn't need another one."

Sophie groans. "I can just imagine what was in your report after everything that happened while you were auditing us."

"I didn't include any of it except to add it to the list of unavoidable injuries and deaths," Carter replies. "Criminal attacks on Fire Department staff outside of work time don't fall under the audit's field of assessment anyway. The only recommendation I could think to make was to post around-the-clock security over the firehouse, the crew's outside activities, and maybe even individual crewmen's personal lives. There was no way I was going to recommend that."

A few people glance up at Duke, but he doesn't respond. He doesn't suggest that maybe we do need security at any of our outside-work events or activities—or that we need security inside the firehouse.

Just then, Zeke, Felix, and a few other kids come over to the picnic table. They start rummaging around in the food for something to eat and discover Duke's bag of fireworks.

"What's this?" Zeke pulls out a giant sword and holds it up.

Emily and Ellen break away to intercept the kids and explain everything to them. The kids won't leave the fireworks alone, so the two mothers set the kids up with a sparkler each.

The kids run off waving their sparklers around, yelling, laughing, having sword fights with them, drawing shapes in the air, and having a wonderful time.

The other adults drift away, either to talk to other people or get their own food.

I end up standing there next to Duke alone. I really need to stop acting so idiotic around him.

He's my boss. I'm going to be stuck with him for a long, long time.

Finding him attractive doesn't mean anything because nothing can ever happen between us. I need to be okay with that and put it out of my mind.

"That was a really great idea—bringing those fireworks," I tell him. "I'm amazed none of us thought of it before."

"How late do you stay at these barbecues?" he asks. "I wasn't sure if you all stay until after dark. It might work better if you used them at night."

I brighten up. "That's a great idea! Sometimes people camp out overnight. It would work out so much better if we did it then. I don't think anyone is planning to do it now. Today was more of an icebreaker....you know....."

"I know. I really appreciate you inviting me. I know it isn't easy for everyone under the circumstances."

I glance up at him and almost get caught in the undertow of his eyes again. I have to stop myself from looking away.

I need to get used to interacting with him. I need to treat him as a trusted friend and advisor the same way I treated John.

"Please don't think it will be like this all the time," I tell him. "This is a really great crew. We all work hard and we care about the job. All this awkward tension between everyone—it will pass in time. It won't always be this uncomfortable."

He turns to face me. Does he feel the attraction, too? "I really appreciate you saying that—and I really appreciate the effort you're putting into making me feel welcome. It means a lot to me that some people are at least trying to ease the transition."

"A lot more people are doing it than you realize." I try to distract myself by waving at the people around me. "People want to accept you and even make you one of us. I think they just don't know how to. They're all still trying to figure out how to transition from John to you. It isn't you. It's them and they know that."

He laughs at that. I take a minute to realize why.

His face lights up when he laughs. His eyes sparkle with life and the wrinkles around his eyes bunch up in the cutest, most adorable way.

He looks a thousand times more attractive when he laughs. I have to control myself not to get butterflies.

He breaks the obvious tension by gesturing toward the picnic table. "Can I get you anything?"

I shoot the table a sidelong glance. "Be careful going over there. People have been known to gain twenty pounds just from looking over there."

He laughs again, and this time, his cheeks actually flush. Is he......Is it possible he's as attracted to me as I am to him?

I didn't mean to make a comment on his physique, but I guess I did. I don't see how a man his age gets to be as muscular, toned, and as strong as he is without working out—a lot.

He jerks his thumb over his shoulder toward the barbecue. "Maybe I should stick with the Roadkill Café instead."

Now it's my turn to laugh. "Good idea."

"Do you want anything," he asks. "I hear the skunk comes highly recommended."

I glance up to make eye contact with him. I'm still laughing and he still smiles down at me the way he did before.

Just for a minute, I sense the chemistry between us building to the breaking point. We're bantering back and forth like we're flirting with each other or something.

Are we flirting? Is that what this is?

I was just trying to lighten the mood. I didn't mean to turn it into something more than that. I haven't said anything to Duke that I wouldn't say in front of John.

I scramble to come up with something intelligent and charming to say. "If you bring me back a nice juicy vulture drumstick, I'll be happy."

He laughs again and crosses the beach still chuckling to himself.

Chapter 9: Duke

I come downstairs from my office and hear the hum of activity coming from the garage. I head for the drug lockup and find the door standing open.

Josh Abbott, Carter Holt, Chris Daniels, and Brooke Elsworth all crowd in there talking animatedly about something.

I frown at them all. "Is something wrong? Shouldn't you all be doing your truck checks?"

"We are doing them," Carter tells me. "Or we're trying to."

"We're running low on glucagon, morphine, epi, and Narcan," Chris adds. "No one has ordered them since John died."

I frown at them all and then glance at the empty section of shelves in front of them. "Shouldn't Keith have ordered them for you?"

"He can't," Josh points out. "You need a special clearance certification to order Class 1 substances like morphine. He was just going through a process of appealing to the State Commission to make a one-time exception. Then you came along."

"I think maybe he didn't mention it to you because he didn't want to tell you how to do your job," Brooke murmurs. "He probably thought someone with your experience would already know about that."

"I was just about to do the order. That's what I came in here to check." I take a step into the locker. Carter, Chris, and Brooke all wedge themselves out of the narrow space so I can get in.

Chris and Brooke leave right away. Josh and Carter stand by while I check the stores.

"Do you have enough to stock the trucks for today?" I ask.

"We're all right for today and we can get more from the hospital when we drop off patients," Josh tells me. "We were just talking about one of us going upstairs to tell you."

I raise my eyebrows at him. "Would you have? Would you have come upstairs to tell me?"

"Of course," he replies. "We were just about to."

I look away. I don't want to say it, but I have to. "I need to know that everyone on the crew will tell me if we need something ordered or fixed. I can't have everyone walking on eggshells and leaving it up to me to find out everything that goes wrong around this place."

"We know that," he tells me. "We were going to tell you. I was going to tell you. I was going to go up to your office and tell you as soon as we finished our conversation."

I glance over at Carter. He stares back at me with the same level gaze he always uses when he looks at me.

I detect a hint of challenge in that gaze. I know the guy's record too well. He's been in a position of authority over Fire Chiefs for years. He wouldn't hesitate to tell any Fire Chief how to do his job.

Carter isn't in that position here, but I can't imagine him hesitating to tell me the drugs are low.

Maybe I'm the one who needs to stop walking on eggshells and reading more into this than is actually here.

No one on the crew would have considered something like this very urgent. They could at least finish their conversation before they stopped work to tell me something like that.

In any other firehouse, they wouldn't have told me until they saw me next. That could have been hours later or even at the end of the shift depending on what else is going on.

I make a note of the missing drugs. "Is there anything else I need to add to the order?" I ask.

"You might want to take a look at the hoses on the two trucks," Carter adds. "They're seven years old and they've seen a lot of wear and tear. They're still perfectly within spec, but I recommended to Chief Brewer to keep an eye on them and maybe replace them. You can decide for yourself whether you want to do that now or keep using them as long as they still have plenty of useable life in them."

I look up at him. "Did you make any other recommendations to him?"

He shrugs. "I guess you can read all that in my report if you really want to know. It was all the usual stuff—nothing staff or management related."

"Except for the whole Andy incident," Josh adds.

"That problem is taken care of, isn't it?" Carter turns back to me. "I would really rather not get into a discussion on the Health and Safety aspects of this department. I'm supposed to be out of the loop on that if you don't mind."

"Of course," I tell him. "I understand."

"Like I said, it's all in my report. I'll tell you if I see anything that concerns me, but I'll do it as a firefighter, not as the department's Health and Safety officer."

"I understand and I appreciate you saying so." I wave behind him. "Let's go take a look at those hoses."

We head out to the garage. My presence doesn't cause widespread panic and anxiety like I expect it to. Everyone keeps working on their vehicles. They're too busy talking to each other to even notice me.

I even hear laughter in the background. This crew is way too resilient not to bounce back from their recent tragedies.

I would like to think my arrival helps grease the wheels for that to happen. Maybe not having any Fire Chief at all made the problem worse. Now everyone can go on with their lives.

Josh and Carter follow me over to the trucks. I put my clipboard aside, but before we can pull out the first hose, the fire alarm goes off.

The crew scrambles into their trucks. No one looks sideways at me while I grab my clipboard and back off.

I take off back upstairs, put my clipboard on the table, and head out to my support pickup to follow the crew to the scene. The order will have to wait after all.

The computer in the support pickup reads out the dispatch notes. The call is a car accident downtown. Two vehicles collided and skidded across the sidewalk to crash into the glass storefront of a florist shop.

The two fire trucks pull out onto the road followed by the ambulances.

I run my pickup around the block to get in front of them on our way into town. I get to the scene first, park my pickup off to one side, and find the Police already on the scene.

They have the area cordoned off with squad cars blocking access. Jim Walker meets me and points to both sides.

"We have those areas there and there roped off for you to park your vehicles. Don't bring your trucks and ambulances in here. There's still a bunch of broken glass and metal fragments all over the street—and the florist had helium piped to nozzles inside. The crash ruptured the pipes. We don't want to risk an explosion."

"How safe is it for my people to go in and check patients?" I ask.

"There aren't any patients inside the shop. All the patients are over there. The two drivers of the cars were both walking wounded and none of the florist staff got hurt. Your people don't need to go into the shop at all."

"Got it. Thank you."

I turn away and meet up with the two trucks just as they approach the cordon. I point up to Keith through the rescue truck's driver window. "Park over there. Don't bring any of the vehicles inside the cordon."

He nods. "Got it."

He drives off and I head over to the ladder truck to give Cameron Santiago the same message. "Park over there outside the cordon," I tell him. "Keep the vehicles outside the perimeter."

"What for?" he asks. "Shouldn't we go inside?"

"There are too many hazards. The Police have that area set aside for you to park. Follow Keith...."

I have to break off when I see Vince Jaeger and Drew Killian both about to drive the ambulances through the cordon.

A bunch of Police officers rush over there waving their hands to stop the two drivers from entering the scene.

Keith, Billy, Carter, Danny, Ellis, Naomi, and Jessie are already unloading from the rescue truck. They stop at the edge of the cordon. They can't get through with all this commotion blocking the way.

I hustle over to the ambulances to give them the same message. It takes a while to get the information across because none of the drivers will listen to me or the Police.

Vince and Drew both lean out their windows to yell at the officers and swipe their hands from side to side to tell the officers to move so the two ambulances can continue to the scene. This is turning into a nightmare.

"Take the ambulances over there!" I tell Drew. "There are too many hazards inside the cordon. Park over there by the rescue truck. That's what these officers are trying to tell you."

"That's all wrong!" he counters. "We're supposed to angle the vehicles on either side of the scene so the paramedics can access the equipment."

"Not this time." I point behind him. "Move the ambulance—now."

I have to race away to the other unit to deliver the same message to Vince. He also protests and I have to go through another agonizing ordeal explaining myself to him.

A yell distracts me. I look up and my world stops when I see Cameron inching the ladder truck closer to the cordon.

The officers are all too busy dealing with the ambulances. No one is there to stop Cameron from driving straight into the scene exactly the way I told him not to.

I spin around to intercept him, but Keith gets there first, jumps onto the footstep outside the driver's door, and yells at Cameron through the window.

I have half a second to see Cameron shake his head and his mouth move. The ladder truck crawls another few inches forward with Keith riding on the outside before the tires hit a metal fragment on the ground.

The front tire explodes and the truck starts to sink on a hissing cloud of escaping pressurized gas.

Keith goes ballistic and yells at Cameron even louder. I get there, grab Keith by the jacket, and pull him off the truck.

"Take your people over there and start treating patients!" I snap louder than I should. "I'll deal with this."

He storms off back to his crew and they walk away toward the patients. Cameron looks down at the dashboard doing something inside the cab.

"Unload your crew and go start treating your patients," I tell him. "Everybody out of the truck."

"I was just following procedure," he counters. "We have protocols for how we position our vehicles...."

I glare at him. "Did you just hear me tell you to unload your crew and go start treating patients? Go do it and don't contradict my orders ever again." I raise my voice so everyone else in his truck can hear me. "Everybody out! Go do your jobs—now!"

I head back to the ambulances. Fortunately, enough Police officers are already over there to stop the two ambulances from making the same mistake.

I have to get harsh with both Vince and Drew before they finally pull their vehicles away and park by the rescue truck like I told them to at the beginning. This is a nightmare. Now I have to unravel this whole disciplinary problem.

This whole thing delays the medical crew from getting to the patients. Carter, Jessie, Chris, and Naomi are already over there.

Josh, Brooke, and the EMTs from the ambulances don't get there until later.

Jessie and Naomi have to stand around waiting for the EMTs to show up with their gurneys before the paramedics can transport critical patients.

None of this would have happened if the two ambulance drivers just listened to me and did what I told them to do.

I have to keep a lid on it during the call. I supervise the crew until the ambulances transport all the patients to the hospital.

It takes a long time because there are a lot of patients. Most of them have superficial injuries.

I wait until the EMTs are on their way out with their last patients. "Come back here after you drop off your patients."

"Shouldn't we go back to the firehouse?" Drew asks. "That's what we always do."

I compress my lips and fight my voice under control. "Did you just hear me tell you to come back here after you drop off your patients?"

He turns a whiter shade of pale. "Yes, Sir."

"Then do it. Get out of here and come back here after you drop off your patients."

He leaves with Brooke and I tell Vince to do the same thing.

I turn around and find the whole rest of the crew watching me. Fantastic. This is the last thing I need.

I should have expected this—and I did expect it. It comes with the territory of breaking in a new firehouse.

This crew's last Fire Chief getting shot doesn't change the fundamental dynamic between us. I have to enforce my authority.

"Keith, Billy, Carter, Danny, Ellis, Naomi, and Jessie—you all ride back to the firehouse in the rescue truck the way you normally would," I order.

"Yes, Sir," Keith replies.

They break away, load up, and the Police direct Keith to back out of the area. He has to maneuver around the ladder truck. It still sits in the worst possible position to block access into and out of the scene.

The ladder truck offers the most damning evidence of Cameron's insubordination.

I've spent the time during ambulance arrivals to call in a team of tire technicians to change the tire on the ladder truck. They're just taking the truck off the jack when Vince and Drew come back with Brooke and Josh.

Now it's time for me to face the rest of the crew. "Brooke and Josh, you two drive the ambulances back to the firehouse. Theo, you drive the ladder truck. Cameron, Vince, and Drew, you're all on administrative suspension as of right now. The rest of you can divide yourselves between the ladder truck and the ambulances and ride back to the firehouse."

Vince gasps. "You're suspending us?! How are we supposed to get back to the firehouse?"

"You aren't going back to the firehouse until I decide whether or not to reinstate you or terminate you for insubordination. All three of you disobeyed my orders and put those patients and your crewmates in danger. You can walk home and take the rest of the day off pending a disciplinary hearing into your actions."

The three drivers stare at me with their mouths open. What the hell did they really expect? The whole call had to come to a grinding halt because of them.

They should have done exactly what I told them to do the minute I told them to do it. Keith did it and he's the most emotionally fragile member of this crew after his brother's murder.

If he can do it, everyone else can do it. I don't see why anyone should be surprised by this.

The rest of the crew stands there gaping at me, too. Only Josh turns away and walks off toward the ambulances to do what I said.

"Go!" I snap. "Go do it."

That gets everyone else moving. The crew loads up and leaves the three offenders standing there with their jaws on the ground.

I wait until the three vehicles safely back out of the area. I don't have to worry about any of them or the people on board. Theo, Brooke, and Josh are way too reliable to mess this up.

I take one last look at Cameron, Vince, and Drew standing there dumbfounded.

They're still standing there when I walk away, get into my support pickup, and leave.

Chapter 10: Naomi

"Did you hear?" Jessie murmurs in my ear. "Cameron is upstairs having his disciplinary hearing with Duke."

"I don't know what Cameron and the others expected," I tell her. "We all heard what Duke said about the scene being too hazardous. All three of those drivers put patients and the crew in danger by not listening to Duke."

She glances over her shoulder toward the other side of the garage. Vince and Drew stand in the corner whispering to each other just like we are.

"Cameron deserves the axe for this," Keith growls from the other side of our group. "I told him not to go in there. He wouldn't even listen to me."

"It's almost like the three of them woke up one morning and made up their minds to stick it in Duke's face," Danny points out. "It was a stupid thing to argue with him about. He got to the scene first. Of course he knew more about the situation than we did. He'd already spoken to the Police about it."

"This is the kind of shit Andy would have pulled," Billy adds. "Andy would have put these guys up to something like this. The son of a bitch isn't even around anymore and he's still poisoning our crew."

"Duke can't fire them," Carter points out. "We're already short-handed. He would have to close the firehouse if he fired all three of them."

Dead silence falls over the group when Cameron comes downstairs followed by Duke.

Cameron's cheeks flame and he won't look at any of us. I gulp when he walks away toward the locker room. Did he get fired? Did Duke send Cameron home on suspension?

No one moves or even breathes when Duke waves at Vince. "Let's go, Vince. Go upstairs to my office."

Vince bows his head so he won't have to make eye contact with Duke on his way to the stairs.

Duke shoots us all a flinty glance before he walks away.

"Damn!" Josh gasps. "Thank the stars I'm not going up there."

"Should we go check on Cameron?" Sophie whispers. "Should we ask him what happened?"

"I'm not going over there," Danny murmurs. "I'm not getting involved in this. I don't care what happened to him. Keith is right. They put Duke in an impossible situation. He has to act even if it means firing people."

"Do you think one of those three is trying to take over Andy's spot as head troublemaker around here?" Brooke asks. "That's the last thing we need."

"You would think what happened to Andy would scare these fools onto the straight and narrow," Carter suggests. "You would think it would bring the crew closer together to make sure nothing like that ever happens again."

"This wasn't malicious," Keith points out. "It was just bone stupid. None of those idiots would have directly disobeyed an order from John if he told them not to drive inside the Police cordon. These morons are just pushing Duke to see how much they can get away with. It's childish."

"Do they really deserve to get fired for doing something stupid?" Brooke asks. "Doesn't Duke understand that we would be resistant to a new Fire Chief coming in and taking over?"

"These aren't children," Keith counters. "These are adults and they're supposed to be professionals. Why do you think the rest of us are cooperating with Duke but those three didn't?"

"I think it was malicious," Danny chimes in. "I don't see any other explanation for it. They deliberately did exactly the opposite of what he told them to do. Cameron had no reason to enter the scene. We didn't even need the ladder truck closer to the florist shop on that call. I could understand why we might have needed the ambulances, but he only did it to spite Duke. That was more than stupid. It was deliberately insubordinate and Duke is right. Cameron's actions did delay essential patient care and put crew in danger. That's enough to get him fired."

Silence falls over the group at those words. I can't argue with anything Danny says.

We're all still standing there in shocked silence when Vince comes down and Duke orders Drew upstairs. Vince has to walk past us to leave the garage.

We see tears in his eyes before he turns the corner and disappears toward the parking lot, but he doesn't drive away. Did he get fired, too? Maybe he just needs to take a few minutes to get himself together.

I can't think of anything to say that we haven't already gone over a million times already. We can stand around speculating about what's going on upstairs. We just have to wait to hear the news.

None of us gets any work done, but we don't really need to. We've already restocked our trucks.

We would be upstairs hanging out in the breakroom if this was any normal shift.

None of us wants to be that close to Duke's office right now. None of us knows what to do with ourselves until Duke tells us the outcome.

I fold my arms and rub them even though I'm not cold. This whole situation makes me shiver. I wouldn't want Duke hauling me up to his office for disciplinary action.

I would have to be blind not to see the way he acted at the scene of that call. The drivers' actions infuriated him—and for good reason.

He's too self-possessed to lose control of himself, but he sure did get harsh with them after it was all over. He didn't say a word until after the drivers delivered the last patient to the hospital. Then he brought the hammer down.

He'll be even harder on the offenders in the privacy of his office. He won't mince words or pull any punches. He has to assert his authority and I have absolutely no doubt that he'll do it.

Drew comes downstairs and goes straight to the bathroom. I heave a sigh of relief. It's over.

I turn back to my crewmates to suggest that we all go back to work. We all freeze when Duke comes downstairs. He crosses the garage floor to where we stand.

"Would you please come up to my office, Keith?" Duke asks.

Brooke gasps out loud, but no one dares to speak or protest.

Keith's face closes up into a brutal mask of silent fury. The rest of us watch in abject horror as Duke follows Keith to the stairs.

"What the holy hell?!" Brooke whispers as soon as the two of them pass out of sight. "Duke is NOT taking Keith in for disciplinary action! He was trying to back up Duke! Keith was trying to stop Cameron from going in there!"

"Don't you get it?" Danny murmurs. "Keith undermined Duke's authority."

"When?!" Brooke husks. "Keith has done nothing but defend Duke since day one."

"That's the problem," Danny counters. "Keith acted as our Fire Chief before Duke came on. Keith supporting Duke undermines Duke's authority. We should be following Duke's lead because he's our new Fire Chief, not because Keith told us to. Duke shouldn't need Keith's support. Keith backing up Duke only weakens his position."

"So Keith is going to get disciplined and maybe fired for trying to do the right thing?" Billy interjects. "He obeyed Duke instantly. Keith never questions Duke."

"This place wouldn't be the same without Keith," Sophie murmurs. "We wouldn't even have Howe Firehouse without Keith Brewer."

Chapter 11: Duke

I wave toward the chairs in front of my desk. "Come on in. Take a seat."

Keith doesn't move. He stands there glaring at the whole world while I shut the door behind him and cross the room to sit down behind my desk.

He's still standing there with smoke billowing out of his ears when I lean back in my chair to look up at him. I've never seen him so furious.

"What is this about?" he snaps in his harshest tone. "Don't think you're gonna pull me up on disciplinary action for trying to stop Cameron from driving into that scene."

"We aren't here to talk about what happened at the scene. We're here because you're overdue for your latest performance evaluation." I wave toward the chairs again. "Sit down, man. You aren't in trouble."

He narrows his eyes at me. "Performance evaluation?! You're serious."

I pretend to check my computer. "You had your last one seven months ago. You should have had this one a month ago, but I guess your brother was too busy dealing with the Health and Safety audit. Maybe he thought he would pick it up after Carter filed his report and your brother dealt with whatever fallout came from that. Audits can be stressful—especially when they involve a lot of interpersonal stuff the way the last one did."

He compresses his lips and glares at me in outright murderous rage. I try not to read too much into that.

This is his way of processing grief. This must be really hard for him—standing there looking down at a stranger sitting in his brother's chair.

He finally looks away, shakes himself, and sits down. He does it way too fast—almost robotically like he wants to get this over with.

Sitting down doesn't relax him at all. If anything, he stiffens even more.

He lowers his head so he can glare at me from under his bushy dark eyebrows.

I look away toward my computer. "Your brother left notes in your file related to your performance ...."

"John did not criticize anything in my performance!" Keith snaps back. "No way can you tell me he put anything in my file against anything I did on the job. He would have told me if he had a problem with me—but he didn't. This is the first I'm hearing about any problem he had with me. If you have an issue with something I did on that call, just tell me now—but you can't give me a poor performance evaluation over one call. That's bullshit."

I lean back in my chair and take a deep breath. I have to be careful with this man.

"I never had any plans to include this call in your performance evaluation, Keith," I tell him. "I called you here to thank you for supporting me—both on that call and every other time. I have nothing to complain about with any of your job performance. Your performance has been exemplary in every respect."

He clamps his mouth shut and refuses to answer. Does he even believe me?

"Ordinarily, I would use the performance evaluation to address attitude and behavior issues, but under the circumstances, the whole crew seems to understand why you're acting this way. It doesn't seem to be causing any adverse effects on anyone else's performance, job satisfaction, or crew cohesion, so I'm going to let it stand for the moment—unless it does start causing any adverse effects."

He shifts his weight in his seat and growls through gritted teeth. "I never had any problem with you, man. Someone has to be Chief around here."

"I appreciate that. You are hands down the most respected and influential member of this crew. My position here would be totally untenable without your support."

He looks away again. He doesn't want me complimenting him.

I turn back to my computer. "As I said, your brother mentioned your professional development in your last few performance evaluations. He recommended you for leadership training and additional professional development that could lead to you becoming a Fire Chief or even a captain. There's also a pay increase involved when you upgrade in rank."

He won't look at me. "I never wanted that. I already told the people at the Health and Safety Commission that I wouldn't replace John."

"I'm not talking about you replacing John. You wouldn't have to work here. You could work anywhere—and you have a wife and baby to think about now. Your brother would want everyone to keep going after he wasn't around to support you all. He would want this for you because it's what's best for you and your family. He wouldn't want you to fall off just because some psycho shot him in the head."

He stares off to the side and mutters under his breath. "I could never leave the firehouse. These people are my family."

"I understand that, but think about it. Something could happen and you might move to another firehouse—or something might happen to me. Then you would be the best man for the job. Even the Commission knows it."

His head snaps around fast. "You wouldn't leave—not when you just got here! You wouldn't go to all the effort of winning everyone's respect just to leave!"

"I'm speaking hypothetically. You going through this training would be the best thing, not just for you and your family, but for the whole crew, even if you never use it."

"I guess I could think about it," he mumbles. "I mean....all right. I'll do it—but only if you don't tell anyone. I don't want anyone on the crew to find out."

"All right, man. I understand. I'll sign you up for it. You can do it in your off time. No one has to find out apart from you and Leila—or anyone else you want to tell. I won't tell anyone."

He glances around. "Is that it? Am I done?"

"Yeah, you're done. You can go back to work now."

He gets up and walks off to the door. I turn back to my computer. Maybe now he'll realize that I'm on his side.

He surprises me by stopping on the threshold and turning back. "Thanks," he clips.

I look up. He makes eye contact for a split second and then leaves.

Chapter 12: Naomi

My friends and I jump out of our skins when Keith comes downstairs from Duke's office. "What happened?!" everyone asks. "Did he write you up?"

"Naw," he replies. "He just gave me my bi-annual performance evaluation."

We all blink at him. "That's it?" Brooke asks. "He didn't... you know...do anything?"

He looks at her and bursts out laughing. "Of course he didn't do anything. There's nothing to do but talk. Performance evaluations are nothing but a bunch of talk."

We all stare at him in shock. This is the first time he's laughed since John's death.

Keith's eyes sparkle with their old light. He doesn't glare and smolder the way he did before.

He acts lighter and more relaxed just since he went upstairs. What did Duke say to him?

"So what are we going to do about Cameron, Vince, and Drew?" Sophie asks.

"We aren't going to do anything about them," Keith replies. "Whatever Duke did to them is what's going to happen to them, even if they get fired." He casts another harsh look around the circle. "You all better treat him with the respect he deserves. He's our Chief now. You all give him the same consideration you would give John."

Just then, Jessie comes back over to us from the other side of the garage. "Could you guys help me out with Ellis? I'm really worried about him."

"What can we do about him?" I ask. "He's still upset about what happened."

"If he won't listen to me, he won't listen to anyone," Carter points out. "I've already said everything I have to say to him."

"What if he does something—like something really bad?" Jessie glances over her shoulder. Ellis sits in a corner by himself. He doesn't engage with anyone unless we go on a call. Even then, he avoids talking unless it's absolutely necessary. "This is so not like him. He's really starting to scare me."

Carter turns around to follow her gaze. "All right. If you think he's that bad, I guess I can try again."

"Thank you so much!" she exclaims. "I just don't know what to do with him anymore."

She and Carter walk away. Keith is coming out of his funk, but Ellis is another matter.

Carter is right. If Ellis doesn't realize that he saved Carter's life, then I don't know what else will convince him.

The rest of us break up to do other things. I meet up with Chris and Josh. He tells us about Duke ordering more drug supplies.

We're just heading over to the locker room when the fire alarm goes off. We have to stop what we're doing and get into the truck.

I'm working in there with Sophie today. Billy heads the dispatch notes. "We got a cave-in under the museum! A school group was down there taking a tour of the old mining tunnels. We got a whole bunch of minor injuries and seven children and a teacher still unaccounted for."

"How secure are the tunnels?" Keith asks on our way out of the garage.

"The city engineers are checking it now. They're bringing in support structures to stabilize the tunnels. All the walking wounded are out of the tunnels and the Police are evacuating the museum."

Just then, Duke's support pickup passes us with the siren wailing. He burns rubber on his way into town to beat us to the scene.

"The guy is no slouch," Billy mutters. "I'll give him that much."

"Just make sure you do what he says this time," Danny calls up from the back seat.

"I was planning to," Keith counters.

We have to work our way through thick traffic to get to the museum. Duke gets there long before us and directs the trucks and ambulances to a section of the parking lot behind the Police cordon.

"Josh, Chris, and the EMTs—get started on triage," Duke orders. "Naomi, Jessie, and Sophie—you go with the fire crew. The engineers will show you into the tunnels—and Carter will be with you in case you need an extra paramedic."

We split up. Keith, Danny, Caleb, Billy, and Ellis join us when we meet the engineers.

Ellis shows no sign of being in danger of not doing his job. That's the weird thing about all this.

He won't say a word to any of us, but he comes back to life as soon as we get a call. He never hesitates to pitch in and help out wherever and whenever he's needed.

I have to pay attention when the engineers lead us into the museum. It sounds spooky with no visitors or even any staff here. This place is usually bubbling with voices.

Duke joins us a few minutes later on our way downstairs to the old mining exhibit. Thousands of visitors come to see this exhibit every year. We've never had a problem with it before.

The engineers stop us at the tunnel entrance. "You're all already wearing helmets, so I don't need to suit you up in those," one of the older engineers tells us. "I do need you to wear high-vis vests and take these handheld radios with you in case anything happens."

He passes out the vests and radios. It takes a while for us to fit our high-vis wear over our SCBAs.

We might not need SCBAs in these tunnels, but I don't want to get caught without it in case one of the cave-ins caused a noxious gas release.

The engineers lead us to the caved-in section of the tunnel. We pass more engineers and construction workers setting up scaffolding and load-bearing jacks to hold up the ceiling along the way.

"This is as far as we've been able to go," the old engineer tells us. "We don't know what you'll find beyond this wall and we don't know where the missing kids are."

Duke comes forward and shows us a diagram of the tunnel layout. "The school group followed the tour route through the red tunnel line here. The teacher shouldn't have taken the missing kids too far away from here."

"How do you want us to do this?" Keith asks.

Duke points up to the top of the rock fall. "There's an opening up there. We'll climb through and see how much of the tunnel is passable. Then we'll just have to explore the tunnel system until we either find the kids or come to another blockage. If you see any sign of instability, pull out and come back here. The engineers will keep working to clear this blockage and support the tunnels. Coming back here should be the safest place if you need to retreat. Don't put yourselves in danger."

"You got it," Keith replies.

"Like I said, the kids should be close to this blockage—unless something happened that we don't know about."

The guys turn away toward the rock pile. We climb up it one after the other to slip through the hole.

The firefighters go first. Keith and Billy drop down on the other side and yell back up to Caleb who lies across the opening.

"It looks stable over here!" Keith calls. "The kids aren't here."

"Keep going," Duke orders.

We all climb through. He comes with us and points off into different side tunnels. "Split up and explore the tunnels. Call out until you find the kids and then bring them back here."

We divide up into three groups with one paramedic to a group. Keith, Caleb, and Sophie go off into the righthand tunnel. Danny, Ellis, and Jessie go straight ahead.

That leaves Billy, Duke, and me to take the lefthand tunnel.

I search the walls and ceilings everywhere we go for any sign of instability. Billy goes in front yelling, "Can anyone hear me?! We're with the Fire Department! We're here to get you out! Call out if you can hear me!"

No one answers him. Duke and I search side chambers on both sides, but we don't find anyone.

"Why would the teacher take the kids so far away from the rest of the group?" I ask after fifteen minutes of searching.

"Maybe something happened to separate them from the group before the cave-in happened," Duke suggests. "Teachers are usually sticklers for keeping everyone together. Maybe they got lost before the cave-in."

Billy calls out again and still gets no answer.

We get to the end of that tunnel and Duke consults his map. "This side tunnel meets up with the main channel. We'll go that way and meet up with Danny, Ellis, and Jessie."

"What about that one?" I point to the map in front of him.

"That's the old drainage channel," Billy points out. "No one goes down there. It's closed to the public."

"Maybe the kids knew about it and decided to break away from the group to explore it on their own," I point out. "Maybe the teacher went to look for them. That could be why they aren't here. It's like Duke said. The kids and the teacher should have been right next to the cave-in, but they aren't."

"I'll get to the bottom of this." Duke picks up his radio and contacts Keith and Danny. "Any sign of the kids on your end?"

"Nothing," Keith growls. "This place is deserted."

"Nothing here, either," Danny reports. "We're heading back to the rendezvous."

"We're going down to the old drainage tunnels," Duke reports. "Pull everyone else out and go back to the surface to finish with triage."

"You got it," Keith replies and hangs up.

Duke leads the way to the entrance to the drainage tunnels. We have to climb down a bunch of stone stairways until we come to a boarded-up archway with warning tape across it.

Hazardous. Do Not Enter.

"This looks exactly like the kind of place I would have liked to explore when I was a kid," Billy mutters.

Duke laughs. "Don't tell me that, man. I have enough personnel problems already."

Billy smirks at him on the side. "I would never do anything like this now—not unless the job called for it."

"Don't act so enthusiastic." Duke takes hold of one of the boards, pulls it off, and creates an opening big enough for the three of us to climb through.

I pass Duke the drug box and the jump kit before I squeeze between the remaining boards.

"If the kids are trapped or confined, you'll be the one to go in and get them," Duke tells me. "Billy and I are the wrong people to go into any tight spaces."

I find myself laughing at him. "I can't wait. I feel so honored."

Chapter 13: Naomi

Billy, Duke, and I set off down the tunnel to search the old drainage channel. This one is a lot darker than the other tunnels. They all have built-in lighting for people to find their way around.

Billy switches on his flashlight and I take mine out of the jump kit. We scan the tunnel on both sides.

It's much rougher and damper. The sound of dripping water echoes from out of sight.

"Can anyone hear me?!" Billy bellows at the top of his lungs. "We're with the Fire Department! We're here to get you out! Call out if you can hear me!"

The three of us stop walking and hold our breath to listen. I don't expect to hear anything here, either, but a faint sound answers us from farther up the tunnel.

We can't see where it's coming from, but someone is definitely down here.

We set off walking faster toward the sound. Billy keeps calling again and again to make sure we're heading in the right direction.

"We're coming for you!" he yells. "Just hang on a little longer! Keep calling out so I can find you! I'm Billy Cates! I'm a firefighter with the

Howe County Fire Department. I'm trying to find you! Where are you?!"

We trace the voice a long way into the tunnel. It drops down a steep slope plunging deeper underground.

We finally emerge in a giant cavern. Who knows how deep underground we are now?

A bunch of voices yell out from directly below us. "We're here! We're right here! Help us!"

Billy and I shine our flashlights downward toward the voices.

The tunnel ends at a rickety, rotten wooden platform hanging by a thread over a high chasm. Our flashlights flicker on an underground river flowing over rocky ledges and falling into pools down there.

We instantly spot the seven kids and the teacher down there. The teacher is a young man with glasses and a thatch of curly brown hair on top of his head.

He's wearing a torn business shirt and he's covered in mud. In fact, all the kids are covered in mud, too.

"We're here!" the teacher calls up. "Get us out of here!"

"We're trying to, man!" Duke calls down. "Give us a second to figure out how to do it. This is Billy Cates, Naomi McFee, and I'm Duke Broebeck, the new Fire Chief. What's your name, man?"

"I'm Gerald Lensky," the teacher replies. "These boys dodged our tour group. I followed them here. I was standing on that platform trying to find a way to pull them up when the platform collapsed under me. I fell down here. We've been down here ever since."

"Okay. Just hold on," Duke replies. "We'll get you out. Don't worry. We know where you are. Just give us a second." He turns to Billy. "We don't have a rope or anything, do we? We might need to send you back to the crew."

I bend over the side. "Is anyone in your group hurt? Is anyone injured?"

"Not that I know of," Gerald replies. "A few of the boys have skinned knees. That's about it."

"I should go," I tell Duke. "You and Billy should stay here."

"No, Billy should go. We'll only be standing around waiting for him to come back and I need you here." Duke turns back to Billy. "Get up there and tell the engineers what's going on. Tell them we need an extrication crew and a rigging crew down here—and bring some more lights."

"You bet. Take this." Billy hands over his axe and a few of his other tools before he walks away up the tunnel. That leaves only one flashlight—mine.

I barely notice that I'm all alone with Duke now. This situation doesn't inspire intimacy if you know what I mean.

He shoots my jump kit a sidelong look. "I don't suppose you have anything in there that could double as a rope."

"Not unless you want to try IV tubing," I smirk at him. "I do have a couple of flares, though."

He brightens up. "Great! Let me have them. Anything is better than this—and we need to save your flashlight batteries."

I unzip my jump kit and hand him three flares.

"I'm going to set off some flares to light the cavern!" Duke calls down to the group. "You'll see a light, but it isn't dangerous. It will just give us some extra illumination to see what's going on."

"Um...." Gerald calls back. "Not to rush you or anything, Chief, but I think the water might be rising."

"It is rising!" one of the kids squeals. "It's flowing faster!"

Duke strikes the first flare and drops it over the side. He aims it so it lands on one of the rock ledges far enough away from the river.

It instantly shows us that Gerald is right. This river must connect up to some outside water source. A surge of water floods the channel and gushes up the side rocks.

Gerald and the kids have to retreat, but the water keeps rising. Gerald and the kids won't be able to retreat forever if this keeps up.

Duke strikes the second two flares and drops them into different parts of the cavern. The water situation gets worse by the minute.

"There!" Duke points over the side. "There's a path leading down across the side wall. We can get down there and bring them up before Billy gets back."

I see what he's pointing at. "It's pretty steep. It's a risk."

"We'll have to chance it. We can't wait for the others. You stay here. I'll go."

"No way!" I tell him. "I'm going with you. You need me."

His head shoots up before I realize what I just said. I contradicted his order, but he doesn't seem to notice that.

His eyes lock onto me with curious power. Does he really need me? I didn't mean it like that.

He turns away first. "We're coming down to get you!" he calls to the stranded school group. "We're going to lead you up a path in the rocks."

We head back up the tunnel, leave the rickety platform, and find the top of the path. It's really steep and only offers a few feet of space between the wall and a sheer drop to the river below.

Duke and I flatten ourselves against the wall. I have to turn my face to the wall so the jump kit sticks out behind me.

We both cling to the wall and inch our way along. Duke keeps looking back at me. "You okay?"

"Yeah!" I gasp. "How much farther?"

"We got a ways to go."

We're too far along for me to change my mind.

The noise of agitation and terrified squeaks coming from the kids gets louder. I don't look at the river to see how high the water is getting.

Gerald's voice rises, too. He's either trying to reassure the kids or.....or something.

Duke and I finally get to the bottom of the path. Gerald is in the process of trying to get the kids across the river to our side so they can join us.

He stands on a long rock ledge jutting over the water. He pulls one kid after another to the edge and practically shoves them so they jump across.

The boys rush us. I steer them toward the path while Duke goes to help Gerald get the rest of the kids across.

There's more space over here on our side. The boys aren't in any danger of getting swallowed by the river, but the water keeps rising.

"Climb up there!" I push the boys toward the path. "We can get high enough away from the water."

I don't tell them that the water might fill this whole cavern. Duke and I need to get these people out of here pronto.

The last two children are the youngest. They flatly refuse to jump across the river no matter what Gerald says to them.

"Pick them up and hand them across to me," Duke orders.

Gerald tries to pick up the first boy, but he's too heavy and Gerald isn't strong enough. He's a young, slight guy with almost no muscle mass.

"Put him down," Duke orders. "Come here, man. Jump across."

He practically pulls Gerald across and then Duke calls me over. "Naomi! Come over here!"

I go over there and Gerald retreats to join the other boys.

"Stand here and take these kids when I pass them to you," Duke tells me.

I nod. "No problem. I'm ready."

He jumps across the river, picks up the first boy, and holds the kid while he thrashes and screams.

"Look at me, son!" Duke orders and moves his eyes right in front of the boy's face. "I'm the Fire Chief of Howe County Fire Department. I'm not going to let anything happen to you. Understand? I'm gonna get you out of here and take you home to your parents. Understand?"

His words calm the boy down just enough for Duke to pass him across the river to me. I grab him and hug the boy. "I got you!" I tell him. "I got you!"

He bursts into sobs and I carry him back to Gerald and the others.

The second boy gets more cooperative when he sees the first boy cross safely. The second boy doesn't fight when Duke picks him up and hands him to me.

I take him away and Duke jumps across to him.

We line up in front of Gerald and the kids to assess the situation. "We can't take them up there without some kind of safety rope," Duke decides—and this time, he shoots me a smirk. "IV tubing definitely won't do it."

I bite back another grin. "Suction tubing won't do it, either. We'll just have to use this path to keep above the waterline until Billy comes back."

We both turn around to measure how far away the water is. It keeps rising, but not fast enough to put us in danger.

Just then, Billy calls down from above. "Duke! Naomi! Where are you?!"

"Down here!" we both yell. "We're here!"

Duke points across the cavern. "There's a path down the rocks over there. Don't come down here, Billy! We need some safety ropes so we can climb up. Don't send anyone else down."

"All right, man!" Billy calls. "Hold the phone and I'll hook you up."

We wait a minute. He retreats up the tunnel and then we see a whole bunch of flashlights bobbing in the darkness.

He comes back to the edge of the platform. "I'm going to throw you down a rope. It's attached to an anchor belay pulley up here. You can lash yourselves together and it will break your fall if anyone loses their footing."

He drops a big bundle of rope over the side. It lands with a thump on the rock shelf.

Duke unravels it and starts arranging it on the ground in front of the kids. Some of them burst into tears of relief when they see the engineers setting up scaffolds and emergency lights in the tunnel up there.

Duke and I work together to wind the rope through the boys' belt loops, wrap it around their waists, and knot together makeshift harnesses to support them.

"All right," Duke tells them. "Start heading up the path. Hold onto the wall. Gerald, you go first." He calls up to the tunnel. "We're coming up! Take in the slack for us!"

"On it!" Billy calls back.

Gerald leads the way onto the path, turns his face to the wall, and clings to the rock while he inches forward.

Duke positions himself in the middle of the group and offers constant encouragement to the boys on the way up there.

I bring up the rear and talk to the boys nearest me. "Keep going," I tell them. "We're going to be okay. We're almost there!"

The boys whimper in terror every time they make the mistake of looking down at the cavern floor. It gets farther and farther away.

The emergency lights cast a haunted sheen over the water's surface. It spreads to cover the whole cavern and keeps rising.

"Don't look at that," I tell the boys. "Look up at the engineers. Can you see Billy? He's holding us up. He'll catch us if we fall. Keep going. We're almost safe."

The rest of the fire crew appears as we get higher. Danny, Keith, and Caleb grab Gerald first and then pull the rest of the boys to safety.

They all collapse panting, sobbing, and moaning in relief. Sophie and Jessie go through the group checking everyone out, but no one is injured.

The engineers start breaking down their equipment as soon as we get there. The fire crew gathers up Gerald and the boys and leads them off into the tunnels to safety.

I sink back against the wall, shut my eyes, and inhale a shaky breath. "Great work," Duke tells me in an undertone. "Thank you so much for your help."

I open my eyes to find him standing right next to me. Billy winds up the rope. The engineers and crew are rapidly vacating the tunnels.

I pull myself together, pick up the drug box I left on the platform, and turn away to follow them. Billy passes us to catch up with the others.

Duke hangs back to walk next to me. I don't let myself think about why.

I feel my legs shaking with relief even though he and I were never in that much danger.

He must notice. "Are you okay?" he asks.

I try to shrug it away. "I've never been very good with heights. They freak me out."

"No one would ever guess. You handled yourself perfectly down there."

I glance up at him, but I have to look away when I see him looking at me.

This is my boss. He's just being nice after that harrowing experience.

He was the one who really handled it. I was just there.

"I mean it," he insists. "Your presence and encouragement made a big difference to those kids. They would have been a lot more scared if you hadn't been there."

I start to say, "I don't know about that....."

A deep rumble cuts me off. The rest of the engineers and crew are fifteen feet in front of us.

We all look up at the ceiling, but the sound comes from somewhere else.

"Everybody out!" the engineers yell. "Move out!"

They charge forward, but those words set off a chain reaction in the rocks around us. One of the walls implodes right next to Duke, and when it falls, the ceiling buckles, too.

He dives out of the way, collides with me, and grabs me before we both lunge backward deeper into the tunnel.

A colossal wall of rock, rubble, and broken gravel crashes into the tunnel right in front of us and cuts off every avenue of escape. Everyone on the crew, the engineering team, and the rest of Howe are on the other side of this wall.

Now Duke and I are trapped in here....alone.

Chapter 14: Duke

I drag my head off the ground and realize with a jolt that I'm lying on top of Naomi with my arms around her.

I get an immediate thrill, but I can't act on it or even show it.

It's pitch dark in here. We don't even have a flashlight to see where we are or what's happening.

I pry myself off her and cough the dust out of my lungs. "Are you okay?"

She coughs and rolls onto her side. "Yeah!" she chokes. "I'm... okay....."

She claws her way onto her hands and knees and then I hear a thump and a scuffling noise followed by a zipper unzipping.

"What are you doing?" I ask.

Something snaps and a bright green glow stick starts radiating faint light into the tunnel—just enough for us to see each other.

Dust covers her hair and clothes. She doesn't look so bewitching now.

She spits dust out of her mouth, wipes her face on her sleeve, and clambers to her feet before she looks around. The drug box sits next to her with the jump kit unzipped on the floor.

We both brush as much of the crap off our uniforms as we can before we both turn to stare at the avalanche of debris blocking our way out of here.

"So much for that brilliant idea," she mutters and turns away. "We'll just have to wait for the others to get us out."

I grab some of the rocks to pull them away, but in a minute, I uncover enormous slabs of granite and concrete. They stack on top of each other all the way to the ceiling. We can't get out that way—or any other way.

She walks away to the other side of the tunnel, sits down against one wall, pulls the jump kit toward her, and starts going through it item by item.

"We have sterile water, normal saline, and lactated ringers. We'll need to ration our water to make it last as long as possible."

I hesitate to turn around. "Do you have to be so practical?"

She snorts at me. "Would you rather I burst into hysterical screaming and uncontrollable sobbing?"

Her snarky attitude makes me turn around and face her. I find myself grinning at her. "Maybe save that for later when we're actually about to die."

"Some nice roasted skunk will probably sound pretty good in a few days."

I laugh. "Hopefully we won't be here that long."

"You might be surprised. If these tunnels are this unstable, the engineers might have to stabilize them first before they dig out this debris. That could take time."

I give it up and go sit down next to her. "Okay, now I really don't want you to be so practical."

She rummages in the kit some more. "We have two Snickers bars. That's our only food. We'll save those for the apocalypse, too."

"What are you doing with Snickers bars in an emergency jump kit?"

"They're for diabetics who need a quick sugar fix."

I make a face at her. "Tell the truth. They're for the paramedics to get a quick sugar fix when one of you gets the munchies. Come on. You don't have to keep any secrets from me."

She laughs—and then she blushes and looks away from making eye contact with me. "We actually have a rule about that. Anyone who snitches the candy bars has to replace them."

"You see? So it does happen. I knew it. I've known too many paramedics in my time. They're the biggest candy snitchers on the planet. They can't keep their hands off any goodies within a ten-mile radius."

She laughs so more. The glow stick casts a haunted light over her hypnotic features. Her eyelashes dip when she looks back down into the kit.

She goes through the rest of it. "We have two emergency blankets and four emergency heating packs for hypothermia. We probably won't have to worry about that down here. These walls will keep the temperature constant."

I glance over at her. She still looks smudged and disheveled after that fall—and all that rubbing against muddy rock down in the cavern.

She still looks beautiful—and her no-nonsense approach to this situation makes her even more appealing.

She's right. I wouldn't want to get stuck down here with a hysterical flutter-budget who weeps and wails and thinks the sky is falling.

She notices me watching her. "What?" she asks.

"I'm glad I'm stuck down here with someone as practical as you—and I'm really glad I had you with me on that call. It makes me feel better that I'm with someone who can handle themselves."

She immediately looks away and pretends to arrange the items in her kit. "Thank you for saving my life just now. I'll never forget it."

"It was nothing. Don't mention it."

She doesn't mention it again. I sure hope she won't start dwelling on it.

I lean back against the wall behind me and start to relax into what could be a very long wait.

The longer it goes on, the more delighted I am to be stuck down here with her and not someone else.

"I've been meaning to thank you, too," I tell her.

Her head shoots up. "What for? I haven't done anything."

"I mean thank you for welcoming me the way you have. It really means a lot—and now....the way we're sitting here talking like normal people.....There's no tension or subtext between us.....It's just natural. Thank you. It's like I actually work here or something."

She makes another face. "You do work here. We're the ones who should be apologizing to you for making things uncomfortable and hostile for you. That was all wrong."

"But you never did that. You've always welcomed me."

She lowers her eyes to her hands and mumbles under her breath. "I'm sure I made things uncomfortable for you, too."

I rocket blast goes off in my mind when I realize what she means. Of course she knows.

The tension between us has nothing to do with hostility or me flexing my authority with the crew.

I don't have to deny the attraction between us. It's palpable and invades every single interaction I have with her no matter how innocent.

Neither she nor I have ever done anything to cross a line. Her behavior toward me has been absolutely professional—or at least attributable to the uncertainty of dealing with a new boss.

"You haven't made me uncomfortable," I murmur low. "I'm flattered that you noticed me."

She doesn't look up. She keeps mumbling in the same defeated undertone. "It doesn't change anything, though, does it? It doesn't matter because Howe Firehouse needs a Fire Chief more than I need a....."

She breaks off and doesn't say what she needs.

I blink at the side of her face, but she doesn't look up. I can't believe we're actually having this conversation.

When would we have it if we don't have it now? We're completely alone here. We might as well lay all our cards on the table before we have to go back out there and face the crew.

"If it was in any way possible, I would jump at the chance," I murmur. "You're....you're delightful. Please don't think it has anything to do with you."

"I get it," she mumbles. "I know you can't—and neither can I. It's stupid even to think about it."

"You can't help who you're attracted to... and neither can I."

Her eyes float up to meet mine. "You mean.....you're....."

I wait for her to finish. "Do you mean do I find you attractive? Of course I do."

She immediately looks away and her cheeks flush. "Oh. I wasn't sure."

"You're gorgeous. Who wouldn't be attracted to you?"

"I don't think of myself that way."

I gasp out loud. "Why not?! You're stunning. Don't tell me you don't have all the guys at the firehouse banging down your door."

"No," she mumbles. "They aren't."

I stare at her in disbelief. She can't be serious—but she must be. She's absolutely drop-dead gorgeous. Any guy would fall over himself just to turn her head.

She distracts herself by zipping up her jump kit and putting it aside. Then she raises her knees and props her elbows on them before she looks around at nothing.

I don't know what to say to her. I want to do something to convince her of how appealing she is.

I flounder through a bunch of jumbled thoughts. Why is she single? Why do the firehouse guys keep their distance from her? Is there something wrong with her?

From what I've seen, she's always been sweet, considerate, outgoing, and competent. She's as dedicated and hard-working as everyone else on the crew.

Out of nowhere, she glances up at me. "What about you? You must have a wife and family somewhere. Are you all moving to Howe together?"

"I don't have a wife or a family. I'm on my own."

Her jaw drops. "You're joking!"

"Nope. I'm flying solo."

She blinks at me with those big dark eyes. I see the same questions racing through her mind.

I can't look at her. I don't want her to see the truth. She couldn't see the truth from the outside, but I still don't want her to see.

I try to turn it into a joke. "Those Snickers bars are going to be a difficult temptation to beat the longer we stay down here."

She blinks again—and then her expression changes. She bursts into another wicked smirk. "I have an idea. You seem like the competitive type."

"Who—me? I have no idea what you're talking about."

She only laughs at me and pulls the jump kit toward her. "I'll make you a bet—or call it a dare. I challenge you, Mr. Bigshot Smarty-pants."

I wind up laughing along with her. "I won't play if you call me nasty names."

She won't stop grinning while she pulls the two Snickers bars out of the jump kit and pushes the kit back into place.

She places the two candy bars on the floor in front of us—both bars equally distant from both of us. Then she leans back against the wall next to me and faces the bars where we can both see them.

"The first person to take their bar loses the bet," she tells me. "I challenge you to beat me."

I glance over at her and I feel my cheeks flame when I grin back at her. "Let me guess. You're the competitive type."

"You're damn right. There is no way I'm gonna let you beat me."

"Then I can't let you beat me, either." I settle back against the wall and face front. "You're on."

We sit in silence for a minute. This bet makes me happier than I have a right to be under the circumstances.

She's right. I'm way too competitive to back down on a challenge like this. This is the perfect way to beat the temptation to eat the bars before we really need them.

Neither of us breaks the silence for a minute. Then she snickers under her breath. "We get to eat the bars as soon as we get rescued. Okay?"

I chuckle back at her. "Deal. We'll just have to eat them at the same time so there's no clear winner."

She shoots me another smirk on the side. "Okay."

I grin back at her. I love that she understands me so well. She really is the best person to get stuck with in an underground tunnel.

Chapter 15: Duke

I jolt awake and struggle to remember where I am. I'm sitting on the floor in the underground tunnel.

The light from the glow stick is starting to fade. I can barely see the Snickers bars on the floor in front of me anymore, but food is the last thing on my mind.

Naomi must have fallen asleep sitting up, too. She's tipped over sideways and her head comes to rest against my shoulder.

I don't move to shake her off. I get a sudden irresistible urge to put my arm around her shoulders and hold her.

These last few hours have brought us closer, but we both still keep each other at a distance.

The feeling of her leaning on me does something to me. I really wish I could take it further with her, but it's out of the question.

I shut my eyes and drift off into the fantasy that there really is something between us.

I imagine what it would feel like if she rested her head on my shoulder, not as a coworker or fellow entrapment victim, but as a lover or life partner.

She's so captivating. She's beautiful inside and out. She's everything I would find appealing in a woman.

Right now, in this moment, when there's no one else around, I can lose myself in the dream that I love her and she loves me. We're asleep here together, not because we have to be, but because we don't want to be with anyone else.

I don't know if I'll ever have that with anyone again. It might be too late for me, but she sure does bring up all those buried feelings.

Neither of us has done anything inappropriate yet. Neither of us has done anything unprofessional.

We're trapped underground. This experience is bound to bring us closer. That's all this is, but I can still dream about it—if not with her, then with someone else.

I'm just about to fall asleep again when she jerks upright out of a sound sleep and gasps out in surprise. "I'm so sorry!" she blurts out. "I didn't mean to....."

"It's all right," I tell her. "No big deal. You can lie down again if you want to."

She doesn't. "I'm sorry. I must have passed out."

Now I really want her back. I want to feel her head resting on my shoulder and even nuzzling against my neck. I don't want to lose that feeling just yet—or ever, actually.

She clears her throat, sits up, and shuts her eyes. "You haven't eaten your candy bar," she mutters.

"Unless I peeled open the wrapper, ate the bar, and filled it with sand so you wouldn't know the difference."

She chuckles without opening her eyes. "Then you're going to get very hungry when we're starving to death and I have a nice juicy Snickers bar to eat."

"Unless I ate your bar, too, and filled that wrapper with sand, too."

"You wouldn't do that," she mumbles with her eyes still closed. "You're too good for that."

I don't want her talking about how good I am when I was just thinking about....her.

"Come lie down on the floor....over here," I tell her.

I move the Snickers bars out of the way. Neither of us needs to see them when we're asleep.

I steer her down on the floor. She lies on her side and uses the jump kit as a pillow.

I fold my arm under my head, and just because, I turn to face her. I move the glow stick in between us so I can look at her face while she sleeps.

I probably shouldn't do this, but the rest of the world can put it down to the last folly of a dying man fantasizing about a woman he can never have.

She lies there with her eyes shut for a minute, but instead of falling asleep, her eyes drift open again after a while.

They lock onto me and she doesn't look away.

We lie here staring at each other—like lovers. Now I know she's thinking the same thing about me

We don't have to say anything. We don't have to act on it. Thinking doesn't hurt anyone nor does it cross any professional lines.

Her body, face, and eyes radiate so much attraction and warmth. I can almost feel her gazing at me.....the way she looked at me in the burning house.

She's gazing up at me in passionate desire. She doesn't try to hide it. She really means it this time.

"You're beautiful," I whisper.

"How are you not married?" she murmurs back. "How has no woman attacked you and dragged you by the hair back to her cave?"

I clamp my eyes shut to stifle laughter. I can't stop my cheeks from burning. "Cut it out. I'm no prize."

"You are!" she breathes. "Do you have any idea how attractive and magnetic you are?"

"You're the one who said you didn't think of yourself that way."

She doesn't joke. Her eyes inhale me with no reservations. "I thought you were some kind of god when you carried me out of that burning house. I thought you were the most stunning man I'd ever seen."

I try to look away, but the depth of passion in her eyes won't let me.

Her eyes dart down to my mouth. "I really want to kiss you right now," she whispers.

"Don't," I tell her.

"I wasn't going to. That would be unprofessional."

I can't answer. I want to do a hell of a lot more than kiss her.

A dying man could be forgiven for going all the way with her as his last act on Earth. I could almost hope I die down here so I can feel her like that just once.

I won't let myself do that, not even in my last act on Earth. We might get rescued in the middle of it. We might get rescued after the fact. Then we would both have to deal with the consequences.

She shuts her eyes. I see her about to go back to sleep. The matter is closed for her.

If she feels any temptation to conquer me as her last act on Earth, she puts it straight out of her mind. She handles this so much better than I do.

I should let her drift off. I shouldn't tell her anything about myself, but this moment flips a switch in my brain.

I'm already sharing something with her—something bigger than both of us. We both want more, but we'll never go through with it. We're both too professional for that, even if it means dying without each other.

"I was married," I murmur.

Her eyes snap open again. She stares at me with that burning intensity.

I gulp to get the words out. "We were really happy together. She was the love of my life. Everything was perfect. I never wanted anything more than to build a life and love her forever. We got pregnant with our first child......"

I break off. I haven't talked to anyone about this—ever. I didn't know it would be this hard.

I realize in that moment that I have to talk about it. One night of ravenous sex might not be the right way to spend my last hours on Earth, but I have to tell someone about this.

It has to be Naomi. I don't know why, but one way or the other, she's the perfect person for me to tell. She's the only person I want to tell and she's right here in front of me.

I feel myself shaking as the words rise to the surface. They won't stop, now that I've already started.

They bring with them a whole tempest of buried emotion. This is why I never told anyone. I didn't want to tap this well of anguish lying buried with the words I never let myself speak.

Without warning, she raises her arm and grips her tiny hand on my shoulder right at the corner of my neck.

She squeezes. It's such an intimate, comforting, innocent act and that touch sends me over the edge.

Tears spring to my eyes, and before I know it, they're streaking down my cheeks.

"It's all right," she whispers. "It's all right."

"She.....she panicked!" I blurt out. "The hormones got to her and she freaked out. She thought the baby was eating away at her from the inside and she thought it was trying to kill her. She had all these hallucinations that the baby was a monster tearing her insides apart. She......." I choke on the words and break down sobbing right in front of her. "She aborted the child and.....and left......"

I'm crying too hard to say anything else. Naomi keeps massaging my shoulder and the side of my neck. She never takes her eyes off me for an instant.

Her steady gaze somehow washes me clean. I don't feel even the slightest hint of shame that I'm breaking down in front of her or that my subordinate now knows my darkest secret.

She raises her arm higher and passes her hand down the side of my face and head. She strokes my hair, my cheek, my ear, and down to my neck.

That touch twists in my guts. She's so kind and comforting. She doesn't have to say a word.

My secret pain is safe with her. She'll never tell anyone—but she doesn't have to because it's all right. She doesn't judge me for it. She understands.

She waits until I stop crying and then puts her hand down. She doesn't continue beyond what's appropriate and necessary.

I drag my face across my shoulder and sniff when I pull myself together.

"Anyway," I croak. "I don't want to get together with anyone unless it's going to be serious. That could never happen between us because we work together. I don't want a casual fling and we could never have more than that."

"I understand," she murmurs. "You won't have any problem from me."

Those words hurt. I won't have any problem from her. I already knew that. I'm the problem—the way I think and feel about her.

I want more with her. It's almost a second betrayal that I found someone I want and can't have her.

Chapter 16:
Naomi

I drift awake to find my head resting on Duke's shoulder again. We're sitting up after another day and night in the tunnel.

The glow stick is completely dead now. It leaves the tunnel plunged into pitch darkness. We can't see anything—or I can't see anything.

Duke's head rests on top of mine. Neither of us tries to keep that professional distance between us anymore. We're stuck down here. We might as well support each other however we can.

His head feels extra heavy. His chest and shoulders rise and fall in deep sleep. He doesn't wake up when I stir.

I try to keep still so I don't wake him up, but it happens anyway. He groans and then shudders in his sleep.

He digs his head a little harder into mine and squirms when he adjusts his position.

I take that opportunity to sit up.

"What time is it?" he growls.

I check my watch. "It's three o'clock in the morning—Wednesday."

Right then, we hear a banging, grinding, and slamming noise coming from above us.

It sounds far away, but it doesn't stop. Then a long, steady vibration buzzes through the rock pile next to us.

Duke stiffens. "They must be starting the excavation. We should move away so we aren't too close to the drill site. The ceiling might cave in some more."

"I'm going to crack another glow stick," I tell him. "We need to drink some of our water before we get too dehydrated."

I rummage by feel in my jump kit, crack the glow stick, and we retreat farther up the tunnel toward the cavern. We sit down at a safe distance where we can keep an eye on the rock pile.

I stuff the two Snickers bars back inside the jump kit. Neither of us is interested in them now.

I take out one of the bags of sterile water, twist off the nozzle, and hand it to Duke. "Drink one quarter of it and I'll drink one quarter of it. That will leave half for us to divide next time."

He takes it and downs a big mouthful. Then he checks to see how much is left, takes a second mouthful to drain it to the quarter mark, and passes it back to me.

I do the same thing. It doesn't satisfy my thirst, but it's better than nothing.

I clamp the nozzle closed with the hemostats from my medical toolkit. Then I put the bag back in the jump kit and zip it up so neither of us will feel tempted to drink any more of our precious water.

We both sit down against the wall and listen to the drilling. It stops after a few minutes. Then another scraping, clanging sound comes through the walls.

The sound keeps getting louder. We can hear engine noise now.

"It sounds like a backhoe," he murmurs.

"How could it be? We're too far underground."

"I don't know how they're doing it, but it's coming too fast. They should break through pretty soon—maybe in a few hours." He smirks at me. "Are you hungry enough to eat your candy bar?"

"I don't care how hungry I get. I won't let you win the bet."

He grins and we both go back to listening to the noise and vibrations. He's right. Whoever is out there is making much better progress than I expected.

We don't talk again. We just sit there next to each other listening.

Without warning, he lowers his hand between us, takes mine, and squeezes. "I'm going to miss spending this time with you. You almost made it a pleasure."

I can't turn that into a joke. I look up at him and feel an overwhelming surge of emotion for him. "I feel really honored that you confided in me. Thank you. You deserve that happiness with someone. I really hope you find it someday."

He looks away. "I don't know if it will ever happen for me again. I might have missed my chance."

"I admire you," I tell him. "I'm really glad you came to work here. Ellen is right. You're the best person to replace John. I never thought we would get another Fire Chief as good as him, but you're proving me wrong."

He squeezes my hand and his voice cracks with buried emotion. "Thank you—for everything. You don't know how much that means coming from you."

He lets go of my hand and faces front. He doesn't say why hearing it from me would mean anything more than hearing it from someone like Ellen.

I don't ask those questions. We both know where we stand.

I can walk away from him knowing that we both did the right thing for each other, for ourselves, and for the firehouse. Life is too good to mess it up by crossing that line.

We sit up and listen for a long time, but the excavators don't break through as fast as we thought.

I eventually fall asleep on his shoulder again and he rests his head against mine.

I wake up in the middle of the night—except that it isn't the middle of the night. Someone touches my shoulder and murmurs, "Naomi—wake up. Wake up, Duke."

I squint into blinding daylight streaming through a hole in the ceiling.

Danny Brewer kneels in front of me with Josh and Carter right next to him. The three guys peer down at me and Duke as we both blink the sleep out of our eyes.

"We're here to get you out," Danny tells us. "Come on. We're taking you out of here."

The two paramedics move in and take our vital signs. "We're okay," I tell Carter when he straps the BP cuff around my arm. "We're just dehydrated."

"You wouldn't want me to get in trouble by not checking, would you?" He puts the stethoscope into his ears.

Josh checks Duke and then the three guys help us stand up.

Duke and I have a hard time seeing in the bright glare after spending three days underground. Danny picks up the jump kit and the drug box.

The guys lead us down the tunnel to the rock pile. The excavators have bored through sections of the street before opening up the tunnel.

A crane basket sits on the tunnel floor waiting to take us back to the surface. All five of us get into it and it lifts us through the hole.

The world looks like a very different place when we get outside. I can't stop staring at everything. I can't believe we're actually out of there.

The basket sets down next to the Howe County Fire Department ambulances. Carter takes me to one of the vehicles and conducts a much more thorough examination on me. Josh takes Duke to the other ambulance.

"How do you feel?" Carter asks me.

"Thirsty....and cramped. We've been sleeping on the floor the whole time."

"Do you know what day it is?"

I glance at my watch. "Wednesday.....four o'clock in the afternoon."

He smirks at me with his misshapen lips. "You cheated."

"You can't blame me for losing track of time."

He drapes his stethoscope around his neck. "You're all right. You can go."

"Thanks, pal."

He smiles at me. "We're all delighted to get you back." He nods at the ambulance. "Get in and we'll take you back to the firehouse."

I have to steady myself before I climb into the ambulance. I turn around to sit down on the gurney. Carter climbs in with me and sits on the bench across from me while he fills out his paperwork.

I recline on the gurney and wind up looking out across the museum parking lot. The excavators drilled through a street behind the building. We were never more than fifty yards away from where we started.

I catch a glimpse of Duke sitting on the back step of the other ambulance. Josh goes through the same series of checks and examinations before he tells Duke to get into the other ambulance.

Duke glances over and sees me watching him. We share a moment of silent eye contact before we both smile.

Then George shuts the door in front of my face and drives off into town.

The ambulance pulls into the firehouse and then reverses into its place. The second ambulance shows up a minute later. The two fire trucks are already here.

The crew crowds around when Duke and I get out. Everyone bombards us with questions. I can't make out much over the noise.

"No, we didn't do anything while we were down there," I reply. "We just sat and waited—and slept a lot."

I hear Duke fielding the same questions and giving the same answers. No one will ever find out what we shared down in that tunnel. I'm not sure I even understand it myself. I don't have to.

Just then, like something out of a distant dream, I see Danny get out of the second ambulance.

He walks around the back and takes out the drug box and jump kit I had in the tunnels. They both came from the rescue truck.

He lays them on the floor, unzips the jump kit, and starts going through it to inventory what supplies it needs. He takes out the bag of sterile water with the clamp on it.

I break away from the crew, go over to him, pull the two Snickers bars out of the kit, and hand one to Duke.

I grin at him and hold out my hand. "Congratulations."

He splits in a matching grin when he shakes my hand. "Congratulations to you. Well played."

We lock eyes on each other as we both tear open the bars and take the first bite. Neither of us will stop grinning. We both watch each other to make sure we do everything at exactly the right moment.

The rest of the crew watches in silence until we both glance around and notice them.

"So?" Duke asks with his cheek bulging. "What's been going on around here?"

"Not a lot," Keith tells him. "I've just been keeping the lights on and coordinating the rescue operation."

"Thanks, man," Duke replies. "I knew I could count on you."

Keith frowns at us. "You know, by rights, you should both take a few days off after an incident like that. I'm the one who will have to fill out the incident report. You can't. You were one of the victims."

Duke only nods. "Okay. I bow to your authority."

Gasps go around the group, but this moment only makes me happy.

Everything's all right between Duke and Keith—which means everything is all right between Duke and the rest of the crew.

Chapter 17: Naomi

I look up from my book and stare out the window at the sun shining on dappled leaves of trees outside my window. The world sure is beautiful, especially after spending three days in a lightless tunnel.

I'm rostered to go back to work tomorrow. Then the usual round of excitement and stress will start back up again.

I wander around my house for a while, but staying cooped up in here for hours on end feels too much like confinement.

I get into my car, drive downtown, and go to the mall. I wander from one store to another looking at all the stuff on sale.

What a bizarre world we live in. All these things seem so frivolous after the days of worrying about such basic survival necessities as water, food, and emergency blankets.

I stop at one of the big department stores at the end of the mall. They have candy and snacks on sale near the register. I buy two Snickers bars to put back in the jump kit.

I stash the bars in my purse and resist the urge to buy two more bars for Duke. Just sitting with him somewhere and sharing a Snickers bar would take on a whole new meaning after the time we spent together in the tunnel.

I go back to wandering around. I don't seem connected to the human race after this experience. No one here knows what I just went through. They wouldn't understand it even if they did know.

Only Duke knows. He knows a secret about me now, too, because he was there with me. We went through it together.

I don't care anymore if anything happens between us. I admire him. I just want what's best for the firehouse and he is definitely it.

Learning his story only makes me admire him more. He's strong, smart, and caring. Who better to take John's place?

I head back in the other direction. I don't want to be among these crowds. I don't want to be around anyone but the fire crew. They're my people—my family.

I tune out what's going on around me. The hubbub of voices fades into the background.

I don't see all the goods on display, either. I don't need any of them. I have everything I need. I just need to get back to work.

A shrill voice snaps me out of my daydream. "Call an ambulance!" someone screams. "Call 911!"

I spin around and see people crowding around a lady sitting on a nearby bench. She's heavily pregnant, leaning all the way back to support herself on her arms, and panting in deep gulping breaths.

A puddle of clear fluid shimmers on the floor under the bench.

People gather around to stare at her like she's some kind of zoo animal or something. I don't see anyone getting on their phones.

I shove my way through the mob to her side. "Get out of the way!" I tell everyone. "I'm a paramedic! Give her some space."

The woman's eyes dart every which way. She seems more terrified of all the people watching her than of actually giving birth.

She lunges for me the minute I show up. She grabs my hand in a bone-breaking grip. "Help me!" she chokes.

"I'm going to help you, Ma'am!" I tell her. "My name is Naomi and I'm a paramedic with the Howe County Fire Department. Don't worry. I've delivered lots of babies and you're gonna be fine."

Her eyes dart behind me. I become aware of maybe a hundred people staring at her.

"Give her some privacy!" I yell over my shoulder. "Go on! Get out of here!"

Three people rush over to us from a nearby store and raise sheets in front of the woman to block her from the crowd. Thank God someone is thinking clearly.

"What's your name?" I ask.

"Mandy...." she whimpers and immediately starts crying.

"It's okay, Mandy. Giving birth is a normal, natural process. Have you ever given birth before?"

She shakes her head fast.

"How far along are you?" I ask.

She glances left and right. The people holding up the sheets hold them high enough so Mandy and I can't see those people anymore. I remind myself to track those people down and give them Snickers bars, too. They're the true heroes of this situation.

I scramble to pull out my phone, call 911, and explain the situation to the dispatcher.

"Yes, Ma'am," he tells me. "We already got three calls from other people at the mall. EMS is en route right now."

I breathe a sigh of relief. The crew is on the way. I just have to hold out until they get here.

"The ambulance is on the way, Mandy," I tell her. "You're going to be fine."

"You don't understand...." she whimpers.

I don't understand because I don't see anything wrong with her.

I place my hand on her stomach to feel how far apart her contractions are. My blood runs cold when I feel her muscles under the skin. They don't relax—at all.

They stay locked in tension. This is not good.

I glance around for some way to deal with this. This baby is coming fast. I don't even have a towel to put under her.

I open my mouth to suggest that I take her somewhere else, but before I can get the words out, she leans farther back on the bench and spreads her legs.

Her eyes widen in a glassy stare of pure terror. Her brain shuts down and she starts pulling up the big dress she's wearing.

She doesn't seem to be aware of what she's doing. My brain shuts down, too. She must be progressing so much faster than I realized.

She pulls up her dress, spreads her legs wide enough to prop her ankles on the bench, and I look down in a daze to see the baby's head crowning right in front of me.

My hands dart out to support it. Mandy grimaces and then shrieks in animal madness. The head pops out into my hands.

As soon as it comes out, she loses all sense of where she is and what she's doing. She rotates forward with the head hanging out and the rest of the baby still inside.

She tries to stand up, gravity pulls the baby the rest of the way out, and it tumbles into my hands. I barely catch it in time to stop it from landing right on the floor.

I scoop the baby up and turn it over to make sure it's breathing. I barely remember to tip its head downward. It's a girl—a perfect, beautiful, wrinkled, discolored baby girl with a fringe of dark hair on her head.

She immediately starts spluttering and crying. I sweep my finger through her mouth—and snap back to reality when Mandy tries to walk away from me.

The umbilical cord tugs when she gets too far away. I grasp the baby tighter, and before I can even tell Mandy to wait, the sheets come down and the fire crew surrounds us.

They bring a whole bunch of Police officers with them. The officers form a blockade around us. Jessie and Sophie grab Mandy and bring her back to the bench. I hear her babbling incoherently, but I can't stop staring down at the baby in my arms.

Brooke comes over to me and wraps a blanket around the baby. The little one's dark eyes trace back and forth searching for something while she cries and moves her little hands around.

"How is she?" Brooke asks me.

I barely look up. "She's fine. She's perfect."

"We cut the cord," she tells me. "You can give her back to the mother."

I can't move for a second. I don't want to give this baby back—because I am the mother.

Every instinct in my gut tells me to keep this child......and put her to my breast.....and take care of her forever. I never want to put this child down—not ever.

Brooke puts her arm around my back and steers me back over to Mandy. She sits on the bench yammering away to Sophie. I can't understand a word Mandy is saying. She doesn't sound like she's speaking English.

Sophie nods and listens intently, but I can tell none of the other paramedics understand Mandy, either.

I bend over in a trance and lower the baby into Mandy's arms.

She reacts instantly by standing up, shaking the paramedics off, and walking away. The Police officers try to stop her, too, but she raises her voice to yell at them and breaks through their barricade.

She strides off through the mall taking the baby with her—my baby. I want her. I want my baby back. She's mine.

Watching another woman walk away with my baby feels all wrong. I should be taking that baby home. I should be the one taking care of her and giving her what she needs.

I'm the one she was looking for. I could have nursed her. I could have comforted her. I could have wrapped her in a blanket and kept her warm and safe and protected.

The other three paramedics pack up their stuff, hold a conference with the Police officers, and break up.

Sophie and Brooke come over to me. "Are you okay?" Sophie asks. "You did great."

I nod at nothing, but I'm not okay. Some stranger took my baby.

My rational brain understands that she isn't my baby, but I still want her back. I've delivered babies before. I've delivered a lot of babies before.

None of them has ever affected me like this. None of them has ever made me realize just how much I want children of my own.

I want to be a mother. I can't stand the thought of going home to an empty house.

I stay coherent just long enough to say goodbye to my friends. I walk them out to the ambulances and I split away to my car.

I drive home in a numb trance. I am going home to an empty house. I can't live like this. This life is a waking death to me.

Chapter 18: Duke

I don't look up from my computer when someone knocks on my office door. "Come in!" I call.

The door swings open. I freeze when I see Naomi in her casual clothes.

She isn't supposed to be here today. She took yesterday and today off from work to recover from her ordeal in the tunnels—but I'm here, so why not?

"Hey! You okay?" I ask and lean back in my chair. "You didn't come to dispute the results of our contest did you?"

She doesn't laugh or even smile. She straightens herself up on the other side of my desk. I've been a Fire Chief way too long not to recognize when someone is about to say something serious.

"I'm here to resign from the Fire Service," she announces.

My jaw drops. "What?"

"I'm resigning from the crew. I'm really sorry to leave you hanging like this. I know you're having enough trouble filling the roster, but I'm out. I'm quitting as of today. I'm not going to work as a paramedic anymore—either here or anywhere else. I'm quitting emergency work altogether."

I stare at her with my mouth open. I don't even know what to say. This is totally out of the blue.

She was fine until the day before yesterday. Did something happen in the tunnels? Did the danger of that incident put her off?

She raises both hands like she has to stop me from protesting. "I know what you're going to say—and it didn't have anything to do with what happened in the tunnels. Just now....a few hours ago.....I delivered a baby in the mall...."

"I heard," I tell her. "I heard it went really well and the baby was healthy and responding well."

She nods. "It made me realize I want kids. I...." She shuts her eyes once, opens them, and locks on me. "I was married once, too. I got pregnant with my first....and I had a miscarriage that broke my husband's heart. He spiraled into a deep depression and it wound up ruining us. I haven't let myself get with anyone since then, but I want to. I really want to be a mother. I'm going to move away from Howe, take a desk job somewhere else, and start looking for someone to settle down with. I don't want you to think this had anything to do with you. You were absolutely right that nothing could happen between us and I respect that. I want you to know I won't lurk around here hoping for something that could never be. You'll be able to keep working here and you won't have to worry about me. It's just....." She shuts her eyes again before she brings herself to go on. "Your story just brought it to the surface. I buried it for a long time, but it's back now and I don't want to wait any longer. I hope you understand."

"I do understand." I stand up to face her. "I'm really sorry to lose you. You're an outstanding paramedic. We're all gonna miss you."

"Maybe you can find a way to explain it to the crew. I'm not sure I can." She steps forward, opens her purse, takes out two Snickers bars, and puts them on the desk in front of me. "These are for the jump kit."

She smiles at me once and walks out. I stare at the place where she was just standing. Then I sit down and stare at the Snickers bars.

Damn, I hate to lose her—and not because of the roster.

I totally understand where she's coming from. I don't blame her for wanting kids. I thought I had it all. I thought I was going to be a father—and then it all slipped through my fingers in a matter of days.

I would give anything to get that back—but I can't. I probably never will again.

I can't begrudge Naomi for wanting to change her life. I know some women keep doing emergency work after they start having kids.

God knows how they do it. I couldn't. I wouldn't want my wife doing it, either—especially not when something like that tunnel collapse could happen.

I turn back to my computer and switch over to the roster. She was rostered for tomorrow. Now we're short another paramedic.

I switch a few things around. I can cover the gaps by moving Carter out of a firefighter position and putting him on Naomi's old shifts.

Just don't ask me how I'm going to explain this to the crew. Maybe I'll take the easy way out and say she just decided not to come back after the tunnel collapse.

I'll say the collapse made her reevaluate what she was doing with her life—which is true. They don't need to know the gory details.

A few minutes later, the crew gets another call. It's a multi-car motor vehicle accident on the highway and takes up the rest of the day.

I get lost in managing the scene and directing the crew in different ways. They work well together, now that the tension between all of us is finally lifting.

I don't have to worry about anyone bucking my decisions.

I get back to the firehouse late and spend a long time in my office filling out the incident report. I still have a lot of work left over from the tunnel collapse, too.

Keith did a great job handling it in my absence. He's going to be great once he gets over his brother's death. He might even take over for me.

I have to go over his incident report, but it's fine.

I take the new roster downstairs and have a conversation with Carter about filling in for Naomi. He doesn't ask any questions and accepts my explanation at face value.

He only nods. "I'm not surprised," he tells me. "Something like that can really make you question the nature of life, the universe, and everything, you know?"

I nod back. "I know. I was there."

"Don't worry about it," he tells me. "I got it covered."

"Thanks, man."

I go back to my office, get my stuff, and go out to my truck to leave for the evening. It's already late and I have to come back here again tomorrow morning.

I'm just wondering if I should crash in the firehouse bunkroom instead, but my body seems to take on a mind of its own.

I walk outside, get into my truck, and drive out onto the street. I'm just turning off to my house when a different instinct takes over. To hell with it. What do I have to lose?

I yank my truck around, hit the gas, and burn rubber to Naomi's house before I give myself a chance to second-guess.

I slam the driver's door extra hard. I'm too determined to back down now or even to question whether I might be making the worst mistake of my life.

I'm not. I know that in the marrow of my bones.

I walk up to the front porch and ring the doorbell. I'm doing this. Hang the consequences.

She answers the door and her eyes widen when she sees who it is. "Hey!" she greets me. "Is anything wrong?"

"Don't leave town," I blurt out. "Stay here...and go out with me. We aren't working together anymore. Stay here. I know I'm old and everything, but give us a chance. We both want it. Don't leave. We can do this."

She blinks at me in shock. "You're serious."

"Yes! Come on. Go out with me." I think fast. "We're having another firehouse barbecue on Saturday. Come to the barbecue as my date."

She gasps out loud and her eyes fall out of their sockets. "You mean...like....in front of everyone.....the whole crew......?!"

"Yes!" My heart feels like it's going to explode. "What do you say?"

She stares at me for a second. Maybe I made a mistake after all.

All of a sudden, she bursts into a huge grin. "Okay! You're on. I'll go."

"Great!" I falter. "Um.....I guess....."

I hesitate. Should I kiss her right now? I came so close to kissing her in the tunnels, but I don't seem to be able to do it now.

I jerk my thumb over my shoulder. "I guess....I'll just....go....I'll pick you up on Saturday....."

She giggles and her cheeks flush. "Okay. See you then."

I take a second to think about it before I can tear myself away. I stand there in stunned shock staring down at her.

I really just did that. I asked her out—to the firehouse barbecue—in front of the crew and everything.

My stomach flips when I think about it. We're doing this. I asked her out....and she said yes.

A moment of sheer terror takes hold of me. Am I really ready to go through all of this again? Can my heart take the strain?

She studies me with the same intensity I'm used to from the tunnels. She waits for me to say something else.

I can't, so I just smile, say, "Bye," and walk away.

I get in my truck before I have a chance to go back up to the porch, grab her, and do something I might regret later. Holy crap! Now what have I gotten myself into?

Chapter 19: Naomi

I can't wait for Duke to pick me up to take me to the firehouse barbecue on Saturday morning. The minute I hear his truck pull into the driveway, I go out onto the porch with two loaded shopping bags.

He hustles up to me grinning like a madman. "Let me take those for you!" He grabs the bags out of my hands.

I giggle in nervous excitement. "Just don't look inside them."

He glances down and his features go slack when he sees a bunch of candy bars in the bags. "You didn't!"

I give an exaggerated shrug. "Guilty as charged. We're going to have to come up with another challenge to see who can go the longest without eating them."

He blushes, smirks, and turns away. "Get in the truck and behave yourself. I might not be your Fire Chief anymore, but I can make life very difficult for you if I have to."

I find myself laughing. "What would you do—force me to eat a candy bar and lose the bet?"

He laughs, too. He puts the shopping bags in the truck bed and opens the passenger door for me. I climb in and buckle my seatbelt.

When I turn around to slot the clip into the buckle, I spot three overflowing shopping bags in the back seat. One of them is full of Snickers bars.

He gets into the driver's seat and sees what I'm staring at. "Great minds think alike, huh?" he teases.

I smile up at him and wind up blushing. "We're both going to be too fat to walk if this keeps up."

He smiles back at me, and right then, he glances down at my body.

I'm wearing a casual pencil skirt, knee-high leather boots, and a small, tight denim jacket with nothing but my bra underneath.

He looks away instantly, but that one look tells me all I need to know.

He only wants something serious. He said so in the tunnels and I already told him I wanted kids.

We can only be getting together for one reason. If this works, we'll be having kids together.

He faces front and drives off into town on the way to the beach. I have a hard time not studying him on the way there.

Am I really going to have children with this man? Why not?

I would have moved to another city and started meeting total strangers in search of a man to settle down with.

I don't need to do that because I already know as much about Duke as I will ever need to know. He's strong, smart, honorable, and very dedicated to family.

He's also extremely committed to being a father. What man would shed tears over losing an unborn child if he wasn't committed to being a father?

He would be a great father. He's authoritative and caring. He was nothing but attentive, gentle, and protective of me in the tunnels. What more could I ask for?

Is he thinking the same thing when he looks at my body? Is he thinking about what it would be like if he got me pregnant?

Maybe he's thinking I might freak out and leave him heartbroken the way his ex-wife did.

I can't imagine anything worse than that, but I feel for her just as much. She must have been in fear for her own life.

The thought of getting pregnant again gives me an excruciating surge of excitement. It almost feels like the pleasure of sex. I almost feel myself peaking to orgasm just from thinking about it.

I don't let myself think about it. Duke and I are on our first date—if I can even call it that.

Don't ask me how we're going to go on a date with the whole fire crew standing around staring at us.

I don't have time to wonder before he pulls into the beach parking lot. We both get out and I lift my bags out of the back.

He takes his out of the rear seat, but he leaves behind the bag with the candy bars in it.

"What about....?" I ask.

"Those are for you." He grins at me. "You didn't think I would share Snickers bars with anyone else, did you?"

I turn bright red. I stop myself from saying that I would get too fat to carry a baby if I ate all those.

I don't say that. I'm not ready to start having that conversation with Duke yet.

God knows why I hesitate. We've already had that conversation. He isn't as smart as I think he is if he doesn't realize the same thing.

He notices my reaction. "So....are we doing the same challenge—whoever eats a candy bar first loses?"

I burst out in giggles again. "Okay. It's a bet."

He grins back at me. "No one can rescue you from this one. You are so gonna lose this time."

"You think so?" Now it's my turn to glance down at his body—at his muscular chest, his chiseled biceps, and his washboard stomach. "Are you on a special diet I should know about?"

"I'm on a no-candy-bars diet," he replies and makes me laugh again.

"I'll just have to find out what your other vices are."

He turns bright red and looks away. "I don't think it will take you very long to figure out what those are."

I could say a lot of things to that, but I make a strategic decision not to and we head down to the beach.

The rest of the crew distracts us when we get there. Duke and I put our bags on the picnic table and join the group standing around in a circle.

"Hey!" Danny exclaims when he sees me. "We heard you quit. We thought we'd lost you to the Dark Side."

I grin at him. "You did. I'm here as Duke's date."

His eyes fall open. "His....date?"

"Yeah!" I can't stop smirking like a moron. "We're going out—now that he isn't my boss anymore."

He gasps out loud. "Is that why you quit—so you could go out with him?"

"No, no!" I counter. "Nothing like that. I quit first. Then he asked me out."

He shuts his mouth with difficulty and swallows hard. "Oh....I didn't know...."

"You're the first to find out—so congratulations."

He keeps gawking at me in blank disbelief. I find myself giggling again. He's only the first of many.

I get the same reaction when I join the circle. Duke is busy talking to Keith and Billy about something related to the oxygen tank order we should have gotten a week ago.

"What's this rumor going around that you quit the firehouse?" Ellen asks me.

"It isn't a rumor. I did quit."

Brooke, Sophie, and Chris all spin around to confront me. "You really quit?!" Chris practically bellows and gets the attention of everyone else present. "We didn't hear that! We thought you were just taking some time off after the whole tunnel disaster."

"No, I really quit."

"You mean—for good?!" Ellen fires back. "Like—forever?"

"Yeah," I reply. "I'm going to do something else with my life from now on. Just don't ask me what I am going to do."

"But you were so awesome as a paramedic!" Brooke exclaims.

I laugh at her. "I'm still awesome. Now I'll be awesome doing something else. I'm not dead."

They all blink at me like I'm speaking another language. They don't understand at all, but that doesn't matter because I understand—and Duke understands.

"But.....will we ever see you again?" Sophie's voice trembles and her features spasm. "I mean.....when would we see you?"

"I'm here, aren't I?" I point out. "I'm still part of the firehouse family, aren't I?"

"Of course!" they all yell at the same time.

"Then I'll keep coming as long as I stay in town. I wouldn't want to miss out on all those nice, tasty skunk burgers."

Duke laughs across the circle. I didn't realize he was listening, but he's the only person who does laugh in the deafening silence.

I glance over at him to see his eyes twinkling and his cheeks glowing when he looks at me. I have to snicker when I see how happy he is.

No one else in the circle moves or makes a sound. They all stare at us as the sinking realization hits everyone.

I see Duke and me acting like giddy school kids. No one understands how things could turn around for us so fast, but it sure looks like this is happening.

The conversation shifts and everyone goes back to talking about something else. No one seems to notice or think anything about the whole me-and-Duke situation as long as they keep talking about the stuff they usually talk about.

I get swept into other conversations. I still have plenty to talk to everyone about, but I realize after a few minutes that most of our discussions center around work.

That's going to change pretty soon—just as soon as I fall out of the loop of what happened on their calls and all the stuff they do at the firehouse.

I won't be the only person who attends firehouse barbecues who has no idea what they're talking about. Other members of the crew have spouses and partners who don't work for the Fire Department—or some other aspect of the emergency services the way Ellen does.

Things will never be the same. In a way, Danny and the others are right about me going over to the Dark Side. It will be kind of like I died to them. That part of my life is over now.

It feels strange to think about it when I look around at all these people I care so much about and who care so much about me.

I know they still care about me. That didn't change just because I changed jobs. I don't regret my decision, but it does make me a little thoughtful when I imagine what things will be like in the future.

We might not have anything to talk about—and I might not come to these barbecues anymore at all. Things might not work out between me and Duke—or I might leave town for some other reason.

I'm standing there looking around at everyone in silence when Duke comes over to me. I didn't realize I'd fallen out of the sphere of conversation before he murmurs in my ear from right next to me.

"Are you okay with this?" he asks.

I glance up at him. I have to smile when I see the depth of care and understanding in his eyes. I also detect a hefty dose of concern bringing his eyebrows together.

"Yeah," I murmur. "I'm better than okay with it. It's just going to take some getting used to."

He inclines his head to one side. "Why don't we take a walk down the beach and talk for a little while? We're supposed to be on a date here and I haven't spoken to you once since we got here."

He holds out his hand to me. I burst into an even bigger smile when I take it. Everyone can see us, but I don't care. It's a good thing that the crew knows we're together.

His hand feels big and warm and strong in mine. My hand feels tiny by comparison.

He squeezes and his expression brightens when we turn away from the picnic tables and head off down the beach.

The kids run around on the sand beyond the picnic tables. Carter brings his surfboard down to the beach. He changes into his trunks, straps the leash around his ankle, and carries his board out into the waves.

All these things are part of the usual barbecue scenery now.

Chapter 20: Naomi

Duke and I walk off heading away from the barbecue. We walk in silence for a while and I become aware that we're holding hands like a real couple.

I don't know how to progress things along or even if I should be trying to progress things along.

He breaks the silence. "Thank you for doing this."

"For doing what? I would be coming to the barbecues anyway if I was still on the crew."

"I mean thank you for giving us a chance. I have a really good feeling about all of this."

I turn to smile at him. I plan to tell him that I have a really good feeling about all of this, too, but when I see the way he's looking at me, I change my mind.

I use walking down the beach as an excuse to look away and face front. "I think we should talk—I mean we should talk seriously—about what this is all about."

"What is it all about—besides us going out together and seeing where it goes?"

I stop in my tracks and face him. "This is what I'm talking about. We already know where it goes. It only goes one place. You said you wanted something serious—which I take to mean you want what you had when you lost your ex-wife. You want marriage and kids and the white picket fence—and I already told you I was quitting the Fire Service so I could find a husband, settle down, and have kids."

"What's wrong with that?" he asks. "We both want the same thing."

"I didn't say there was anything wrong with it. I'm saying we need to talk about it so we both understand that we're only going in one direction. The only reason I'm going out with you right now is because we're both going in the same direction."

"Then that's a good thing, isn't it?" he asks. "What more is there to talk about?"

I take a deep breath and blurt out what's really on my mind. "I'm not on any form of birth control. I just want you to know right now. If we ever had sex, I could get pregnant. I probably would get pregnant. My ex-husband and I had a discussion about us starting a family and I got pregnant that same evening—so I just want you to know I'm not likely to have any problem conceiving. I just want you to know—because it seems like you have an idea that we're going to explore this and see where it goes when that isn't likely to happen at all."

He frowns down at me for a minute. "Oh. I see what you mean."

"The only way we could explore this and see where it goes is if we never had sex. I'm not saying I'm opposed to that. I just want you to understand. If we ever did it, we would be doing it knowing I could get pregnant. So we would have to decide whether we're both ready to go there with each other."

He won't stop furrowing his brow at me. I can't tell if he's rethinking his whole approach or just taking in everything I'm saying.

I straighten up and face him. "How do you feel about all of that?"

He studies me for a second and his features don't clear. "You're right. It's a lot to think about, especially when we just started going out."

I hesitate and then blurt out. "I have a really good feeling about this, too. Everything I've seen from you so far tells me I really would love to go there with you, but you seem to want to take things slower and see how it goes."

He doesn't say anything right away. I break the tension by turning away and tugging his hand so we keep walking.

He walks in silence for a while. I might have blown things with him by saying all of that, but I don't regret it.

If he backs off, I won't have lost anything. I still have my plan in place to move to another city and start over. I can walk away from him.

I don't want to. The longer this goes on, the more I'm really starting to hope he's the one I do it with.

He's such a magnetic, attractive, attentive man. He has such a beautiful heart.

He walks on in silence without breaking it. I'm prepared to walk all the way to the end of the beach and back to the barbecue without saying anything. He obviously needs to think about what I said.

We pass the headland to a different part of the beach. We're the only people here. It's much quieter here, now that we can't hear the kids and traffic.

The surf lulls me into a daydream. It's so peaceful here.

I drift away into another world—a world that doesn't have anything to do with emergencies and danger and all the stress of my former life.

What a different life I'm going to be living from now on. I didn't realize just how different it would be until right now.

My life as a Fire Department paramedic looks so frightening and unnecessarily stressful from the other side of this decision.

Why did I risk my life and put myself through that for so many years? I didn't need to. It was completely unnecessary.

I did it to help people and save lives, but in a way, I sacrificed my own life to do it. I put my own happiness on hold and maybe even ruined it—for what?

The life waiting for me feels much easier, happier, and more fulfilling. I never thought I'd see it that way. I always thought my job made my life as fulfilling as it needed to be.

This quiet moment brings it all back home. I made the right decision. I don't belong in the Fire Service anymore. I can't imagine myself ever going back to it, now that I've tasted what life on the outside will feel like.

We get all the way to the end of the beach. Rocky cliffs cut us off from going any further. We're almost a mile from the barbecue. We have no choice but to turn around and walk back.

The waves boom against the cliffs. Sea birds screech overhead and the wind makes a howling sound over the plateau up there.

I slow down as we approach the rocks. Duke slows down, too.

I expect him to turn around and walk back in silence, but instead, he pulls me to a stop and faces me.

He lets go of my hand and cups both hands around my cheeks. His eyes become deep and intense when he looks deep into my eyes.

"I really appreciate you saying everything you said just now," he tells me. "You're absolutely right.....and I think we should take things slow. We should take the time to get to know each other and make sure we both really want to do this—with each other, I mean. We both know we want to do this, but we don't really know each other well enough to decide if we want to do it together."

I'm already pretty sure I want to do it with him, but before I can say that, he bends in and kisses me.

He brings my lips to his mouth in a soft, gentle, ultra-romantic kiss that doesn't venture past the surface.

He doesn't try to jam his tongue down my throat or take it any deeper than this.

He eases back and gazes into my eyes from close range. He doesn't take his hands off my cheeks. His eyes soften even more until they shine with depth and emotion.

"I wanted to do that so bad when we were in the tunnels," he murmurs. "I wanted to do so many things with you then."

My throat tightens when I remember our time in the tunnels. All the aching connection and feeling of that time comes rushing back.

I wanted to do so many things with him then, too—and they didn't have anything to do with sex.

I would have liked to go all the way with him then, but I mostly wanted to put my arms around him and love him. I really felt like I could in that moment of bare truth and total exposure.

He kisses me one more time the same way, eases back, and straightens up to face me. He doesn't let go of my face.

"I just want you to know," he goes on. "I want to say categorically for the record—that I really, really want to go there with you. I'm speaking only for myself here. I understand if you don't feel the same way—but I want to do this. I would do it with you right now even knowing you could get pregnant. I would marry you and have kids with you and the white picket fence and everything. We might have only been going out for a little while, but I know enough about you to satisfy myself and I'm all in. I'm ready to go whenever you are. All you have to do is say the word. I know I'm probably not what you're looking for....."

"Why would you say that?" I interrupt. "Why do you keep saying that? You're exactly what I'm looking for."

He opens his mouth to answer and frowns again. "I am?"

"Of course! Don't you understand that by now?"

"But.....I'm like....fifteen years older than you are."

"So what? You're healthier than ninety percent of the guys my age. You're gainfully employed...."

He bursts out laughing. "That isn't anything exceptional. I'm sure there are millions of men out there who are better off than I am."

"There aren't millions of men out there who are as dedicated and honorable as you are. There aren't millions of men out there who are as caring and hard-working and committed as you are. There aren't millions of men out there who could have gotten through that tunnel collapse with as much humor and level-headed maturity as you did."

He makes a face. "I had a lot of help with that. I had help from the best."

"I want to do this, too," I tell him. "I'm ready to go whenever you are. I don't see anything in you that would make me hold back. I'm all in, too. If you said you wanted to take it slow and get to know each other to decide if this is right—if you said that to give me an escape valve—I don't need one. I'm ready to go and I want to do this. All you have to do is say the word."

His eyes fall out of their sockets and he stares at me in what looks like horror. His voice cracks in a shaky undertone. "Are you serious?"

I nod even though he's still holding onto my face. "I'm absolutely serious."

He stares at me for a second before he lets go of my face, turns away, and sets off up the beach again. He takes my hand first, though.

He must not have been as ready as he said he was.

I'm prepared to continue all the way back to the barbecue in silence. I don't want to intrude on his thoughts. I want to give him as much time and space as he needs to wrap his head around all of this.

Chapter 21: Naomi

Duke doesn't go back to the barbecue. He heads up the sand and sits down at a distance from the waves. He pulls me to sit down next to him.

He stares out at the waves for what seems like a long time. I should probably ask what's on his mind, but I already know. Now the ball is in his court. It's his turn to make the next move.

I throw caution to the wind, let go of his hand, put my arm around him, and rest my head on his shoulder. I haven't done that since the tunnels.

It means something so much more now. We're together—or we're going to be, one way or the other.

He feels strong and warm and comforting like this. He feels exactly like a man I could crawl inside and live the rest of my life there. He feels exactly the way I want my future husband to feel.

I felt it in the tunnels. Now we're here.

I hope our whole relationship is like it was in the tunnels. I want him to be the shoulder I lean on when we're in danger and I need to feel someone strong and solid and immovable sitting right next to me.

He responds the same way by tilting his head to the side and resting his head against mine the way he did in the tunnels. He feels perfect like this, and just to seal the deal, he turns his head and kisses my hair into the bargain.

Then he nuzzles his head down on top of mine. I sink into this feeling. I can weather any storm as long as he's here. We can face any disaster and get through it together because of this bond.

He's everything I'm looking for. I know that now. We share something already. No amount of time spent thinking about it and questioning it will ever make me change my mind about this.

Time will only make this bond stronger.

I could spend the rest of my life just sitting here next to him with my arm around him, but in a minute, he stirs, turns to me, and kisses me again.

He doesn't give me a chance to realize what he's going to do. He raises his head, and when I do the same thing, he cups my cheek with one hand and brings my lips to his mouth in a much deeper, more passionate, succulent kiss.

He sinks all the way into me this time. His lips collapse against mine. He turns his head to one side and then his mouth opens.

His hot, delicious tongue slithers into my mouth and sets my world on fire.

My hands fly to his face and shoulders and hair. I can't stop touching him.

He feels the way he felt in the tunnels. I touched him then, but only platonically.

All those feelings erupt back to life. We're kissing the way we both wanted to kiss then. The walls come down.

We aren't exploring anything here. We both move in on each other with no holds barred.

He wraps his arms around my torso to pull me toward him, but our positions sitting on the beach make it impossible for us to get near each other.

We're both kissing so maddeningly and we don't pull apart when he lifts me up and swivels me onto his lap. I don't know what he wants, but I wind up straddling him.

We can't stop kissing as though our lives depend on it. I can't kiss him enough.

I can't taste enough of his mouth and drown in the softness of his lips. His tongue electrifies my body and tickles me all over.

I attack him in desperation. I want to do it with him right now, but for some reason, it doesn't ever go as far as that.

He kisses me back just as hard. His hands touch me all over. He pushes my hair back from my face, cradles the back of my neck, rubs my back, and crushes me in his arms to pull me tight against him.

I cling to him with all four limbs, but this is just kissing. Neither of us escalates. I don't know why because we obviously both want to.

His heat infects me until I tremble with excitement. My body quivers with so much pent-up tension, but some invisible barrier stops both of us from releasing it.

Neither of us slacks off at all. Duke hugs me tighter as our kisses build in panting desperation until he falls back on the sand with me on top of him.

We don't ease off even then. I can't stop kissing him and he keeps running his hands all over me without ever trying to get past my clothes.

He can touch more of me here. He squeezes my hips and gropes around to my ass. He pulls me down in an obvious suggestion of doing more.

That's when I feel how rock hard he is between my legs. His package digs into me through my pants.

He pulls me down on top of it and I arch my pelvis to grind on him, but that's all. Rubbing against each other like this turns me on beyond belief. I feel myself spiraling out of control and I whimper in ragged need.

My sounds set him off. He claws at me harder and faster, but he doesn't try to take my clothes off. He never touches my breasts or venture between my legs.

He grabs my thighs, crushes them in a massaging grip, and steers my hips down onto him harder.

His breath catches in his nostrils every time I ride down on him. His package strains and throbs against me, but it's the rest of his muscles that really light my fire.

His big arms, chest, and shoulders consume me and overshadow me. He dominates me in size and strength. My desire doesn't touch the granite power of him.

He grabs my ass again, and this time, his fingers creep just a little lower toward the crease between my legs. He doesn't actually touch me, but that grip and the obvious hint of more sends me spiraling out of control.

I crush his rod with all my weight and dissolve in a wicked orgasm that overtakes me way too fast.

I crumble still locked against his mouth.

He grabs me so fast he surprises me. He cups the back of my head to hold my mouth against his. His ravenous kisses devour my tortured screams and he drives up into me from below.

I'm already tumbling head over heels into the sweetest climax I can remember. I buckle in his arms and ride it out.

I would scream out loud if he let me, but in a minute, he pulls off my mouth, sits up with me in his arms, and steers my head down on his shoulder.

I can't stop moaning and whining as the waves of blissful torment sweep me into another world.

I shut my eyes against his neck and sob out all the longing and blissful pleasure pouring out of me right now. I don't know where that came from. I must have been keeping it bottled up for a long time.

He kisses the side of my face, rakes his fingers through my hair and rubs my body while I power down. I hold onto him with all my might to steady myself in this storm.

He cradles me in silence until I sink into his arms in a daze. All the energy drains from my body. I can't move or even think. He doesn't try to make me.

I might even have dozed off, because when I come back to my senses, I'm still sitting here on Duke's lap with his arms around me.

He shows no sign of wanting to stand up. He just holds me and gazes out at the waves while I pull myself together.

He hugs me tighter when he feels me stirring. I don't want to get up just yet. I nuzzle into his neck and shut my eyes in the safety of his arms. I don't want this to end.

He doesn't seem to want it to end, either. He turns his head and kisses me on the side of the temple.

"Sorry about that," I mumble.

"It's a blessing to have you on top of me like that," he murmurs. "You can cum on top of me anytime you want to. It's a privilege for me."

I clamp my eyes shut to hold back a sudden surge of emotion. Of course he would see it that way.

It's a blessing and privilege for me to feel how hard he gets and to be able to crumble with his arms around me. His arms and body feel like the greatest blessing of my life.

That's nothing compared to his heart, though.

I finally work up the energy to raise my head and shake my hair out of my eyes. "We should probably get back."

He only smiles at me. "You definitely need a Snickers bar now, don't you?"

I snort. "You just want to make me lose the bet. You can't trick me with sex. Nice try, though."

He laughs. "That bet wouldn't have lasted five minutes if we fooled around in the tunnels. We would both have been too hungry afterward."

I find myself grinning. I can finally function now when he lifts me off his lap and we both stand up.

Chapter 22: Naomi

D uke and I brush the sand off our clothes, take each other by the hand, and set off back toward the barbecue. We have a long way to walk and neither of us is in any particular hurry.

"Can I ask you something?" he asks after a few minutes.

"Sure. Anything."

"You said you had a miscarriage," he begins. "Did you have a health problem that caused it?"

I wince. "I don't know how much I should tell you."

"Tell me everything. I need to know everything if we're going to do this. It could affect us. I need to know the risks going into it if something like that could happen to us."

I cringe again. "You're right. I'm sorry. I wasn't trying to keep anything from you. It's just....."

He glances down at me. "It's what? Tell me. Now I'm worried."

"You don't need to be. I didn't have a problem. My husband did—my ex-husband. I was six months along when the baby spontaneously miscarried for no apparent reason. It was really a stillbirth because the baby was almost completely developed. He just needed to grow a lot. We were both devastated when he died. The hospital offered to do a forensic autopsy on the fetus to find out what went wrong. We both said yes because we were desperate to make sure it didn't happen again."

"So what did happen? What were the results?"

I take a deep breath. "My husband had a genetic disease he didn't know about. We found out afterward that his mother had more than ten miscarriages before, between, and after having two children who actually survived. My husband carried the gene which caused our son to die mid-term. That's what really sent my husband into a downward spiral. It completely crushed him to think he was the one who caused our son to die the way he did."

Duke falls silent. "I am so sorry about that. That sounds awful."

I squeeze his hand. I find myself getting choked with emotion when I look up at him. "I'm really sorry about what happened to you, too. That sounds like an absolute nightmare."

"It was." He looks away. "It was by far the most painful thing I've ever experienced."

"I want you to know I never went through anything like that," I tell him. "I was over the moon about being pregnant. I have never felt better in my life. I felt strong, healthy, happy, and I couldn't wait to be a mother."

"Thank you," he murmurs. "You don't know relieved I am to hear you say that."

I find myself looking away across the waves. "In a way, I felt like being pregnant was my most perfect state—like my whole life was supposed to be lived in that state. I completely shut down after the miscarriage. If I hadn't shut down, I would have gone off and started looking for another husband as soon as my first marriage ended. I should have gone straight out and started looking for a man who could get me pregnant again so I could get back to that state as soon as possible—but I didn't do that. I spent months trying to convince my husband to get me pregnant so we could try again, but he wouldn't even look at me. He got it into his head that he could never go through that again because he didn't want to be responsible for another child's death. I never wanted us to split up. I still loved him more than anything. I kept trying to work it out right up until the day he walked out on me. I couldn't stand that feeling of not being pregnant anymore, so I had to shut it down. I had to completely cut myself off from that feeling so I could function. That's the only reason I waited so long to try again."

I trail off and realize with a jolt that Duke is standing there staring at me. I turn bright red and try to look away. "Sorry," I mumble. "I shouldn't be rambling like this."

He only stares at me in amazement. "It's incredible to hear you talking like this. I've never heard anyone talk about it with such....such enthusiasm."

I look away, but he can already see my cheeks blazing. "Sorry. I may have said too much."

"No," he murmurs. "I feel the same way. I just never met anyone who had the nerve to say these things out loud. I thought I was the only one."

I look up at him. "What do you mean—you feel the same way?"

"I mean....it's like I have this biologically programmed drive to get a woman pregnant. I know that's normal and probably every other man on the planet has the same thing, but no one talks about it. I feel like all the rest of this is just window dressing until we get to that—almost like none of this means anything unless and until we're doing that. I felt......when my wife was pregnant.....exactly the way you just said—that this was the way she was supposed to be and it was my job to keep her like that always and forever with no break in between.

I understand rationally that it isn't possible. I'm just saying from an instinctive, biological perspective. I absolutely loved the way she looked and felt when she was pregnant. She was intoxicating like that. Just knowing she was pregnant and watching her body change—it was the greatest aphrodisiac I've ever felt—and I felt like I was supposed to be like that always and forever, too—like it was my job to be a father always and forever and never let myself slip out of that state." Now it's his turn to look away. "My life completely fell apart without that."

I squeeze his hand one more time. "You sure pulled it together. You didn't let yourself fall off a cliff. Believe me. I know. I've seen what happens when a man falls off a cliff."

He glances at me and his expression changes in a heartbeat when our eyes meet. "Let's go swimming!" he exclaims.

I frown at him. "What?"

"Let's go swimming! Come on! We're at the beach. Let's go!"

He yanks off his jacket and then his shirt. I go through a moment of dizzy vertigo when I see him with his shirt off for the first time.

He's absolutely jacked to the limit. His uniform and the rest of his clothes usually hide his size. They definitely hide the definition in his muscles.

I forget what's happening for a second when I see how chiseled his arms, shoulders, chest, and stomach are.

Just in case I thought he wasn't serious about this whole crazy swimming idea, I have to put my doubts to rest when he rips open his pants, pushes them down, and kicks off his shoes.

He's wearing black lycra boxer shorts under his pants. He throws his clothes on the sand, bursts out laughing, and takes off running for the waves.

Before I know what's happening, he dives headfirst into the surf, breaks the surface, and whoops out loud before he starts stroking his powerful arms out into the deep water.

"Come on, Naomi!" he yells across the water. "Come on, chicken! I'm gonna know you're a snowflake if you don't come!"

I find myself giggling. He knows me too well. I could never back down from a challenge like that.

I throw caution to the wind and start pulling off my clothes. To hell with it. What do I have to lose? So I'll get a little wet.

I strip down to my bra and underwear, race down the beach, and I don't let myself hesitate before I dive in.

I get a face full of salt water, break the surface, and start swimming through the waves, too. I can't stop laughing from sheer exhilaration.

Duke whoops again when I get near him. He rears out of the water, dives headfirst into a coming wave, resurfaces, and catches a wave to body surf toward shore.

He only makes it a dozen yards before the wave tumbles him over. He goes down laughing and I find myself joining in.

He doesn't come up right away, so I stroke over there to make sure he's okay.

He resurfaces right in front of me, bursts out laughing when he sees me, and then turns aside to see if any more promising waves are coming his way.

I do the same thing. An enormous wave is almost about to break on top of me, so I dive under it and swim through it to the other side.

I come up to see Duke body surfacing again. He sure can swim with those long, powerful arms of his. He catches the wave and biffs it, but he only laughs.

He comes up behind the wave as it crashes into the shore. He swims out to join me and has to dive under a few more waves to avoid getting caught by them.

I tread water and turn around to squint across the ocean. This is the first time I've swum in the ocean in a long, long time—maybe even since I was a kid.

Duke breaks the surface near me just then, tosses his head to shake the water out of his hair, and whoops again. "Whoo! This is great!"

He beams at me.....and our eyes lock. We're both smiling from ear to ear, but that look stops the world. It stops time. It even stops the w aves.

We float in a timeless dimension where nothing exists but the two of us.

I keep treading water. I lose track of how long I stay in one place. I bob on the waves that keep rolling past me.

The same waves make Duke rise and fall at the same time, but I don't notice that. This man.....we're actually going to do this. We both want to.

My stomach flips when I think about building a future with him—and seeing him every day—and handling all the minutiae of daily life—and raising children with him—and managing all our finances—and facing all the challenges that come with integrating our lives with each other.

I read the same truth in his eyes. He's scared, excited, and determined all at the same time. He knows what going together in the same direction means and he wants that. He wants it more than anything.

Chapter 23: Naomi

Out of time, Duke swims the last few feet to me, wraps his arms around my waist, lifts me against his wet, powerful body, and starts kissing me for the ages.

I fall on his mouth devouring everything about him that I've just seen written in his eyes. I can't get enough of it or get there fast enough. I want it all right now.

He lifts me out of the water and I wrap my legs around him in rabid passion.

He attacks my body much harder than before, grabs my ass in a crushing grip, mauls my breasts, and slides his hands down my back to the slot between my legs.

We both pant hard into each other's mouths, but we don't shut our eyes when we kiss. I never want to stop staring into those eyes. I don't want to lose sight of the future we're going to build together.

He keeps his eyes open the whole time. His gaze drills me with its intensity. He's doing it. He's making it happen just by looking at me.

My body responds off the charts to his touch, his lips, his presence—everything he does blasts me to kingdom come.

His crushing, massaging hands feel normal groping all over me. This is right. Everything that happened before is wrong.

He grabs my breast through my saturated bra, and without warning, he plunges his hand down behind, does something to his shorts, pulls my panties aside, and stabs in with brutal ferocity.

I gasp in shock, but he's already inside. The orgasm I had on the sand prepares my channel and makes me soft, juicy, and sensitive.

He glides right in with no resistance and I immediately collapse in another earth-shattering climax.

I can't stop staring at him as the waves of pleasure take me. He drives in again and again. His arms clamp around me and shove me down on his thick shaft to propel me out of this world.

He gasps through bared teeth and his nostrils flare with every rasping breath.

I can't take my eyes off him as we both spike into ecstasy and his hot load floods me in seconds.

Our bodies lock in an unbreakable hold as we both crest an epic climax. He flexes every muscle to drill into me with mind-blowing power.

I couldn't touch the ocean floor just now, but he must be able to. He doesn't have to tread water to hold himself up.

He pins me against him with both arms strapped behind my back. His chest, stomach, and hips arch into me in wicked, penetrating thrusts that deliver his load deep, deep into my forgotten being.

As soon as it's over, our mouths come together in the same blistering kiss. I can't stop kissing him even as his shaft pulsates inside me.

Those spasms hold me trembling on the tip of another cataclysm. Little bursts of ecstasy keep popping off in front of my eyes and electrocuting through my body every time his muscles flex.

I don't know when the moment comes. Nothing changes between us except that we both pull apart, pull our clothes into place, and start swimming for shore.

We climb up the sand, get dressed without a word, take each other's hands, and head off down the beach.

I wring the water out of my hair, and in a minute, my clothes dry me enough that I don't feel uncomfortable even in my wet bra and underwear.

All that pleasure dulls my senses. I don't seem to be able to think about anything on our way back to the barbecue.

We get there to find the beach deserted. Everyone is gone. We must have stayed out longer than we realized.

We go straight to Duke's truck, he opens the door for me, and shuts me in before he drives off on the way back to my house.

I don't know what to say to him or even if I should say anything. That was like no other date I've ever been on in my life.

I'm not sure what to think about it or if I should think anything about it.

He pulls into my driveway, shuts off the engine, and gets out to open my door for me. He takes my hand and leads me up to the porch before he turns to face me.

"Thank you for a wonderful first date," he murmurs. His eyes glow with so much depth and meaning.

I start to smile—and immediately change my mind.

I take a step toward him, rise on my tiptoes so I can reach him, put my arms around his neck, and start kissing him again. I don't want to stop—ever.

He responds by wrapping his arms around my waist and lifting my feet off the floor so we can kiss at his level.

He kisses me ravenously, passionately, endlessly. I let my eyes sink shut in the deep vacuum of just being near him. I don't need to think or decide anything. This is right. What else would we be doing besides kissing?

He keeps going for a long time before he puts me down, but he doesn't stop. He keeps kissing me, stroking my arms and back, squeezing my neck, and lacing his fingers into my hair to keep my mouth locked with his.

He finally pulls away and stands up. His eyes tell me he doesn't want to leave, but he thinks he has to.

I go through another moment of tossing aside all restraint. Why are we following these rules? Rules don't apply to us.

I take his hand, turn aside, push open my door, and then turn backward to stare up at him when I draw him across the threshold. I swing the door shut behind him. He's in my house—where he belongs.

We rush each other kissing faster and more furiously. Screw it. We just did it on the beach. I want to do it again. I want to do it a million times. I don't want him to leave—especially not when we both just said we wanted this.

My body stretches to the breaking point. Everything we've been doing gets me primed and ready. I can't come down now. My desire spikes off the charts and becomes insatiable.

He comes at me just as hard, and in seconds, he starts pulling my clothes off.

I rake at his jacket and shirt just as fast. I want my hands on that body. I want to feel his strength pumping into me. I want his skin exciting me and taking me.

He yanks my jacket open, rips my bra down, and grabs my breasts in brutal, pinching, twisting squeezes.

I yelp into his mouth, but that only seems to spur him onward.

I pull up his shirt, but I can't get it off fast enough. He's too big and his face glues to mine in deep, molten kisses.

He breaks away just long enough to strip his shirt off. Holy Christ, he's big! His powerful physique towers over me rippling with muscle—and then he's on me.

He flicks my bra off and throws it and my blouse away. He grabs me, lifts me up into the same position I was in when we did it in the water, and buries his face in my chest.

I scream when he sucks my nipples in rabid madness, but he only does it for a second before he raises his face to kiss me again.

His hands rove all over me, squeeze my ass, massage my slit between my ass cheeks, and even plunge down the back of my skirt trying to touch me.

I don't know what we're going to do or how we're going to do it. I only know I have to do it with him right this minute before I lose my mind.

He turns aside like he wants to glance around the living room. He changes his mind, takes one step toward the nearest wall, and pins me against it.

He pushes my skirt up, shoves between my legs, and his hardness takes my breath away. The pressure on my slit propels me into another rapidly escalating spiral to the stratosphere.

He pulls off my mouth for a second and I see his features transformed in feral madness unlike anything I've seen from him before.

His hair falls over his eyes. I don't recognize the heat and power blazing in those eyes. He's not the man I thought he was. The considerate, professional Fire Chief isn't here anymore.

He tries to unzip my skirt, but he can't do anything with my legs around him.

Before I know what hit me, he lowers my feet to the floor and attacks my skirt in a storm of fury.

He pulls it the rest of the way up, but I can't get around him again like this. He plunges in to kiss me again. I try to keep up with him, and at that moment, he slithers his fingers between my legs and feels how wet I am.

I moan into his mouth just begging him to finish me off, and just as fast, he turns me around, shoves me face downward against the wall, and crushes me from behind.

He twists his face and mouth around my head while his body pulsates behind me. He shoves his hard package into my ass—and then he leans back just long enough to yank open his fly.

He drills into me from behind. I scream out—or try to. His mouth muffles my screams—and then he's all the way in pumping me to oblivion.

I scream all my passionate release into his mouth and feel my own tortured juices gushing around his shaft as I peak again and again.

He pulls my hips back into his thrusts, flexes his knees to drill into me from below, and his strained breath billows into my nose every time he pants in excitement.

His power drives me up the wall and blasts me into such an epic torrent of rapture that I can't stop climaxing.

Just when I think I can't take any more of this, he circles my waist with one hand, fingers my clit with tiny, cruel little circles, and sky-rockets me into outer space.

He uses that one hand to lift me into his thrusts, angles my ass backward to meet him, and spanks in with delicious, brutal thrusts.

I can't kiss him anymore and I don't have to. He rips off my mouth and I really start screaming as soon as he releases me.

He bites my shoulder, mauls up my neck, and husks in my ear with each beastly pump of his rigid shaft.

His weight holds me down. Just in case I wasn't sure who was in charge here, he plants his hand against my back just below my neck.

That hold spirals me out of my mind. He has me. He's taking me exactly the way I want him to—and then he erupts another torrential load of his seed into me.

He's doing it. He's taking my body and making it his. He's making me the ripe, fertile, succulent fertility goddess he wants me to be.

He snarls in my ear and even bites me in animal madness as his molten essence floods me. I can't stop myself from climaxing on that thick rod pumping into me. I want to milk it for every drop of seed he can give me.

He powers down before I do. He slows his thrusts and his guttural snarls in my ear turn to deep groans of satisfaction.

I'm still quivering and trembling with so much power and energy when he glides his fingers out from between my legs and eases back enough for me to stand up.

He leaves his hand planted against my back until the very last minute, He doesn't release me until he wants to. He keeps holding me down to let me know that I'm his.

He's the one doing this to me. He's the one planting his seed in me. He's the one taking command of this whole situation.

Chapter 24: Naomi

I lie against the wall gasping, moaning, and whimpering as endless surges of excruciating pleasure keep rushing through me. I don't know how to function after everything Duke is doing to me.

The power of his presence makes me tremble more than anything. I feel my life falling into his grasp, but that's the way it should be. I want to. I want to feel that I'm trembling and electric with pleasure from everything he wants to do to me.

He doesn't try to get me to turn around right away. He kisses me from behind, crawls his scorching mouth down to my shoulder and behind my neck, and then bites the back of my neck in such a canine way that I scream again.

I want him to attack me like that. I want him to reduce me to an animal in heat for him to impregnate.

He pulls off my jacket and bra from behind without turning me away from the wall. I shut my eyes, lay my face against the cold plaster, and plant my hands there in the throes of so much passion. I can't move away from this one solid point of focus—not yet.

I feel his hands all over me. He gropes my breasts from behind, slides his hand up between my thighs from behind, and stirs his fingers through our combined wetness dripping from my engorged slit.

He sighs in satisfaction when he feels how wet I am. Then he starts pulling my skirt and shoes off.

He bends down to pull them off. He doesn't tell me to turn around. I don't know what he's going to do right now, but I want him to see me like this. I want him to see me exposed and surrendering to him.

He hitches my skirt down to my ankles and slides my legs out of it. I'm just wondering what he wants to do next when he takes hold of my hips and spins me around to face him.

He knees behind me and winds up in front of me. He's too close for me to get off the wall, and before I know what hit me, he buries his face between my legs.

I gasp and then shriek as his mouth lights me on fire all over again. I flatten myself against the wall, but he's already taking over again.

He grabs my ass to pull me into his mouth, and in one masterful maneuver out of some kind of fevered dream, he lifts both my legs over his shoulders.

He stays kneeling there in front of me with my legs around his head. He takes all my weight on his shoulders and even lifts me off the floor as he devours me.

I scream staring down at his eyes blazing between my legs—and then I explode in another reeling climax.

I feel myself bucking against his face, but he only doubles down and eats me faster.

He plunges his fingers into my already quivering channel and packs me so full that I have no choice but to climax again and again.

He controls my movement and also the distance between me and the wall. I arch back so just my shoulders rest against the wall. He supports all my weight on his shoulders, but that only causes my weight to shove me down harder against his face.

I ride him harder, but that only encourages him. He buries his whole face in my flesh, shuts his eyes, and roots all the way in.

I can't think or even see straight anymore from all the rapture he's giving me. I could keep going like this forever and he doesn't show any sign of slowing down.

My screams turn to plaintive sobs of pure ecstasy. I can't hold back. This avalanche of sensation and emotion flooding through me takes over. I couldn't stop now if I tried.

He makes the decision for me again—thank God. He eases back to little teasing licks and pulls his saturated fingers out of my glistening channel. Every nerve stretches me to the breaking point. The slightest touch sends me crashing over the edge into another screaming climax.

He powers down. His licks become lighter and gentler, but he still teases me to ragged insanity with that cruel, hot, masterful tongue of his.

He eventually eases my feet to the floor. I almost fall over in a drunken haze. I don't know what's happening to me. I've never felt this much pleasure with anyone.

I barely notice when he kicks off his shoes again and pushes his pants and shorts all the way off.

I snap back to reality when he takes hold of my thighs, lifts them both off the floor again, wraps them around his waist, and plows straight back into me.

I can only stare up at him in the depths of intoxicated madness. His body owns me in ways I can't even describe. My channel shivers all around him, ripples down his shaft, and spasms to drive us both wild.

He slams me back against the wall again, pulls me away so only my shoulders rest against the solid surface, and holds me there watching my body contort and arch for his pleasure.

He rides up against my ass a dozen times until he feels me responding to him.

Just as fast, he scoops me up, lifts me in his arms still impaled on his iron shaft, and kisses me while he holds me against his chest.

His breath strains with tension and insatiable desire. His mouth attacks me and his tongue invades my mind as never before.

I sob in bliss on his powerful, impaling spike. I can ride down on him like this and drive myself to another blistering crescendo.

He adjusts his hold on me so I can arch and grind at the angle that suits me best. He growls at me when I crush him inside me. His voice strains each time I take him in and then he sucks air through his bared teeth when I pull off for another thrust.

He scoops his hand up my back to my neck, pulls me in for another devouring kiss, and then turns away to carry me out of the living room. We didn't make it more than a few feet inside the front door before we tore each other's clothes off.

He crosses the living room before he realizes he doesn't know where to go. He tries to kiss me and look around at the same time. "Where do I go?" he asks.

I nod toward the side hall leading to my bedroom. "Over there." Then we both burst out laughing at the ridiculousness of it all.

His eyes crinkle up and twinkle at me while he carries me down the hall. We walk into the bedroom and he bends over to lower me onto the bed.

Things turn deadly serious when he crawls onto the bed with me and I spread my legs to take him all the way in. I sprawl in front of him while props himself over me and stares down into my eyes.

Neither of us can deny anymore that we both know exactly what we're doing. I can't even remember how many times he's unloaded into me today. Now he's about to do the same thing again.

His washboard abs and powerful chest contract each time he drills his thick rod into my puffy, swollen channel. He knows what secrets lie in there and he knows what will happen when he ejects his seed into me.

He's doing this deliberately. He does it knowing the consequences—for both of us.

He stares down into my eyes and I stare back. I see the same future written there that I saw in the waves, but it's different this time.

His face spasms with so much exquisite emotion. He worships me like this. He aches for the life I can give him and I ache and worship him for the same reason.

His rock-hard body, his veiny meat pounding into me, his hip bones slamming me to another mind-blowing climax—my heart twists with so much love for everything he's doing for me.

I want to be his aphrodisiac. I want to be the fountain of fertility that makes him strong and vital and so, so masculine.

He wants me to be the feminine equivalent of that and now he's making me into that. His seed will take me over. It will change me into something I don't recognize.

He stays above me and holds eye contact all the way through it this time. He doesn't fly off into animal madness or quicken his pace at all. He drills into me with slow, deliberate, masterful strokes.

He doesn't stop even when my vision slips out of focus in a shattering climax that leaves me convulsing and writhing underneath him.

He keeps corkscrewing into me no matter what. He can destroy my body in the best possible ways.

My eyes float back into focus just long enough to see him watching me disintegrate in front of him—and then, without warning, he picks up the pace to a rapid, galloping hammer blow that ends in one deep, brutal strike.

He gasps once and his whole being quakes as his shaft bulges and erupts into me. He never takes his eyes off me when he fills me to overflowing with that hot, sticky, blistering seed.

Chapter 25: Duke

I wake up in the middle of the night and feel my arms around a woman. I go through a moment of wild terror when I try to remember where I am and how I got here.

Just for a minute, I think I'm back with my first wife and we're going through the nightmare of her disastrous pregnancy.

This woman in my arms is way too small to be her. This woman in my arms is tiny, petite, and she smells different.

A faint glow from a streetlamp outside gives just enough light to show me that I'm in her bedroom. We both passed out in here after hours of non-stop sex.

Her smell floods me with memories from the beach, the tunnels, and even the burning house where I first met her.

I shut my eyes and sink into the bed in the dark. It's all right. I'm with Naomi.

She heaves a shuddering sigh in her sleep and gives a very small noise like a squeak before she drifts off again.

She lies facing away from me with her small body spooned between my arms, chest, and legs. My bent thighs rest against her ass and thighs from below.

Her body feels magical and intoxicating like this, especially when I think about how many times I unloaded into her yesterday and all night last night.

I drift into a hazy state half awake and half asleep. All our conversations from the beach come back to me.

She knows so much about me. She knows more about me than anyone—and yet we barely know each other.

I could take her again right now. I could cup her breasts from behind and slide between her juicy, swollen petals. I could feel her damp, succulent walls clamp around me and her inner muscles just begging for my load—my seed.

Thinking about getting her pregnant makes me so hard again, but I determine to lie still and let her sleep.

My body has other ideas and she stirs again when she feels me stiffen.

Before I can stop her, she extends her arm behind her and takes hold of my shaft in her tiny, wicked little hand.

She grips it hard enough to make me gasp and my blood rushes into it until I'm straining against her fingers.

Before I even know what hit me, she steers it into her from behind. My stomach contracts on its own and I thrust in.

She mews in an agony of desire, and before I can even move, she pushes herself up and away from me.

She props herself on her arms with all her dark hair spilling over her face, arches her back, and angles her hips down to take me all the way inside.

I watch in stunned disbelief as she climbs onto her knees and drives back down on me in brutal, wicked pumps. She takes me in deep and hard and true.

She spreads her knees wide with her glorious, magnificent ass pointed right in my face. I don't have to do anything but lie here while she grinds on my spike and throws her head back in a husky, animal snarl.

Lust and passionate madness transform her into a goddess of the night. Her curved sides, her swollen breasts, and her rounded ass sway, thump, and spiral in front of me while she straddles my shaft and penetrates herself on me.

My hands migrate forward with a will of their own. They trace her curves and follow her movements in the dim light.

She intoxicates me with her insatiable passion and blatant enthusiasm for everything we do. She never slows down. She never hesitates. She never questions.

In a matter of minutes, she winds herself up to another squealing orgasm and her juices gush around my shaft to bathe me in her magic.

She tosses her hair to one side, gives me one feral glare over her shoulder, and then her eyes roll back in their sockets.

Her lips shiver with ragged breath. Her face, chest, neck, and nipples flush with hot blood and her inner muscles stroke me beyond my wildest dreams.

She spirals her hips on top of me even after she starts to wind down. Her energy is like nothing I've ever experienced.

I sense her de-escalating. She'll sink back down on the bed and fall back to sleep. I should let her, but I don't seem to be able to stop when it comes to her.

I discard all pretense of controlling myself, rotate onto my knees, and pull her hips against me so she winds up on all fours.

She screams when I thrust into her, but a second later, she tosses her hair aside and glares at me over her shoulder again.

The look in her eyes sends me out of my mind. I plunge into her so much harder, faster, and more brutally than I ever have before. I slam her hard and her juices spatter her ass when I spank in against her soft flesh and thighs.

The harder I go, the more she seems to enjoy it. She throws herself back into my thrusts and bares her teeth at me.

I can't stand seeing her so out of her mind with desire and passion. My body reacts and unloads into her all over again.

My guts hurt from doing it so many times and I collapse instantly, but she doesn't leave me alone.

She crawls on top of me, drapes her delicious body over me, and undulates on top of me to excite herself.

I'm too exhausted to do anything, and pretty soon, she powers down and wilts in a sagging puddle of magnificent rapturous sleep.

I jolt wide awake for no apparent reason, but I'm still in bed with Naomi. She's slipped off me and clings to me from the side.

Her delicate arms surround my chest and her witchy dark hair spills over my arm and shoulder.

Every part of her feels like a benediction. Just one hair of her head touching me makes me want to weep with so much relief and happiness, but I can't lie here and enjoy it.

I can't roll her over and make her scream again—much as I would like to.

Sunshine streams through her bedroom windows. The clock on the bedside table says, *5:36 AM*.

I have to go to work today. I especially have to go to work today after the two of us disappeared from the barbecue yesterday.

I peel myself out from under her, sit up on the edge of the bed, and cradle my head in one hand. I really need to think.

I could have gotten her pregnant last night. I really should have thought that through, but it's too late to go back on it now.

I don't want to go back on it now. I wanted this. Now I'm getting it.

I'm still sitting there rubbing my temples when her soft hand comes to rest on my back. "Are you okay?" she murmurs.

"I'm fine," I mumble under my breath. "I'm just thinking."

"Are you okay with all of this? You aren't having second thoughts, are you?"

"I'm not having second thoughts." I heave a massive sigh. "I just need to catch up with the whole thing."

"Do you want to take it slow after all? Is it too fast? We can slow down if you aren't ready. I could go on some kind of birth control......"

I have to turn around and face her. I can't let her think I'm doubting any of this. "No! I want to do this....I just want to do it right. I want us to be properly married—and we aren't even really dating. I want.....well, you know what I want. I just...." I find myself running my fingers through my hair again. "I just need to get my head straightened up. I don't want to change anything. I just haven't caught up with the present yet."

She studies me with her head on one side. Her eyebrows twitch together in the center. She's worried about me.

I bend over and kiss her. "Don't worry. Everything's fine—and everything is still on. We're doing this. Everything is going to work out."

She wraps her arms around my neck to kiss me. I have to tear myself away so I don't get sucked back into her charms.

I sit up, but even looking at her offers a temptation almost too powerful to resist. It's a damn good thing I don't have to work with her anymore. I wouldn't be able to concentrate.

"I have to get ready for work," I tell her.

"Of course," she replies. "Do you want to take a shower?"

I nod. "What are you going to do today?"

"I don't know." She glances around the room and I realize for the first time that a stack of moving boxes lines one wall across from the bed. She's been packing up to move—or she was before I asked her out.

"You aren't still thinking about moving, are you?" I ask.

"Well....I might have to—if we move in together—won't I? I don't know what to do—and if I get pregnant, I won't be able to take a job. I don't really know what I should do."

"We should talk about that and make a plan," I tell her. "If we get married, I'll support you and you can stay home with the slugs."

She bursts out laughing. "You bastard! How dare you call them that?!"

I can't help kissing her again. "I'll keep you in all the Snickers bars you can eat." I stand up and head for the bathroom. "You just have to admit defeat. Then you can stuff yourself and get as fat as you want."

She laughs as I disappear into the shower. I have to stop myself from thinking about her.....and everything.

I take my mind off it by deciding what I'm going to do when I get to the firehouse. Heaven knows I have enough to cope with—and now I'm down another paramedic.

I get out and get dressed to find Naomi in the kitchen making breakfast for me. "How do you like your coffee?" she asks.

"I don't drink it. Thank you anyway."

Her jaw drops. "You can't be serious!"

"I can't stand the smell. I don't understand how people can drink that sludge."

She throws up her hands. "That's it. We're finished."

I laugh at her. "I'm not saying you can't drink it."

She smirks at me over the kitchen counter. "You like Snickers bars so I guess I can give you a pass just this once. Just tell me you like pineapple on pizza."

"Hell no!" I counter. "I'm Italian. Only psychopaths like pineapple on pizza."

She frowns at me. "Broebeck is a German name."

"Don't confuse me with details. I'm Italian because I say I'm Italian. I identify as Italian."

She bursts out laughing. "Yeah, okay, pal. Keep telling yourself that. We'll order separate pizzas—one for you and one for me."

I have to smile at her before I kiss her goodbye. "I'm relying on your honor that you won't sneak out and buy any candy bars while my back is turned. We're carrying out this bet on the honor system."

She snorts in my face. "Says the man driving around with an entire bag of candy bars in the back seat of his truck. Who do you think you're fooling?"

I really need to leave, but I can't tear myself away from joking around with her. "I bought forty candy bars. You can count them when I come home from work each night."

She raises her eyebrows. "Forty? You said you were on a no-candy-bar diet. What happened to that?"

"I haven't touched those candy bars. I told you I bought them for you."

She grimaces at me. "Well, I am never going to lose that bet. Those candy bars are going to rot uneaten in the back of your truck before I let you win."

I laugh. "Famous last words. I gotta go. I'll call you later."

I kiss her one more time and get out of there as quickly as I can.

Chapter 26: Duke

I stop by my house, change into my uniform, and get my game face on when I pull into the firehouse parking lot.

I have to keep reminding myself that no one here knows what Naomi and I did last night. Everyone saw us walk away down the beach holding hands.

No one knows anything else and they aren't going to find out. I'll be damned if I let anyone here find out that we're talking about getting pregnant, getting married, and having a bunch of kids together.

I put last night as far out of my mind as possible—and this morning—and all of it. I need to keep my worlds separated or I'll start getting hard again right here in the firehouse.

I walk into the garage and see everyone busily working on their truck checks. Everyone greets me, wishes me a good morning, and a bunch of people smile at me. Things are turning around.

I go upstairs, check my email, field a few phone calls, and go back downstairs. The crew stands around shooting the breeze like they usually do.

Only Ellis sits off by himself looking in the other direction. He never talks to anyone now. No one goes over to him or tries to bring him into the group. They're all sick of trying and I don't blame them.

I've been keeping a close eye on his job performance. He conducts himself perfectly on every call. He does exactly what he's supposed to do, obeys all instructions, and he couldn't be more helpful.

He just never talks to anyone. He barely makes eye contact.

"What's the word, Chief?" Danny asks.

"Let's pull out the hoses from both trucks and check to see if we need to order new ones."

"Didn't Carter already do that?" Billy asks.

"He did, but he isn't the Chief in charge of this firehouse, is he?" I wave toward the rescue truck. "Let's go. I want to get this done before you get another call where you have to use them."

Everyone gets to work. Ellis must have been listening because he comes over to help pull the hoses out into the driveway.

He works with the same energy as the rest of the crew. The others talk enough so that no one would notice how quiet he is.

I don't really notice it, either. He's been like this for as long as I've known him. I've never known him any other way.

I hear plenty from the rest of the crew about how worried they are about him, but I can't do anything as long as he continues to perform.

I'm not sure doing anything or staging some kind of intervention \ would be best for him. I don't know what's best for him.

We stretch out the hoses and lay them flat before Carter and I go over them in minute detail. He points out all the spots that caused him concern in his Health and Safety audit.

The rest of the crew follows us and watches and listens to our conversation. We also inspect the nozzles on both ends of all the hoses. We connect them up to the nozzles on the trucks to make sure everything is still working the way it should.

"I don't see anything wrong with them," I finally tell him.

"Neither did I," he replies. "I didn't recommend to Chief Brewer that he replace them and I'm not recommending that you replace them. I just told him and I'm telling you that they aren't as young as they used to be. Most firehouses would have replaced them by now, but most firehouses would have caused a lot more wear and tear on them than we have. I just wanted to draw it to your attention."

I nod and frown down at the hoses. "I'll have to keep an eye on them."

"At the current state of wear and tear, they could last until your next audit," he points out. "You could wait until you're due for another audit, replace them, and go into the audit with brand-new hoses."

I smirk at him. "You're going to be a very useful guy to have around, aren't you? It's a good thing you aren't supervising our new Health and Safety officer."

His misshapen lips twist the wrong way when he smiles back at me. "I'm just telling you what I know."

I turn away to tell the other firefighters to put the hoses away when a car pulls up in front of the firehouse.

It parks right across the driveway—right where it would block the trucks from getting out if we had a call.

I can't ignore that, but before I can tell the person to move, a woman gets out of the driver's seat. She leaves the engine running and she's holding a newborn baby in her arms.

I realize as soon as I lay eyes on her that she must have been driving behind the wheel while she held the baby in her arms. She didn't keep the child in a car seat the way she should have.

That on its own is a major motor vehicle violation—not to mention a red flag for child neglect.

My hackles rise, but I don't even get a chance to greet the woman before she hustles up the driveway coming straight toward me.

Her wild eyes dart all around the crew without seeing anything. "I need to see Naomi!" she blurts out. "I need to see Naomi right now! It's an emergency!"

"Naomi isn't here, Ma'am," I tell her as calmly as I can. "Is there something I can help you with? We're all trained in emergencies here." I glance down at the baby. It looks healthy enough.

The baby's glassy dark eyes trace back and forth not looking at anything, either. The baby looks calm at the moment.

"I need to see Naomi!" the woman insists. "I need to see her right now! I have to see her!"

I open my mouth to tell her again that Naomi isn't here and that, whatever her problem is, the rest of us are just as qualified to deal with it as Naomi is.

I keep thinking there must be something wrong with the baby, but the little one doesn't make a sound.

Right then, Sophie steps forward. "You're Mandy, aren't you?" Sophie asks. "Naomi helped you give birth at the mall, didn't she? I'm Sophie...and this is Chris....We were there with you. Do you remember?" Sophie's eyes dart down to the baby. "Is everything all right with your daughter? She looks beautiful."

Mandy shakes her head fast. "I can't do this! I can't do this!" She paces back and forth for a second and then, before any of us realizes what's happening, she rushes me and shoves the baby into my arms. She blurts out one more time, "I'm really sorry! I can't do this!" and races back to her car.

Keith jumps up and runs down the driveway. "Hey! Stop!"

Mandy doesn't listen. She dives behind the wheel, guns the engine, and screeches off down the street.

Keith runs after her yelling, "HEY!!"

Mandy doesn't stop until she skids around the corner and disappears.

I don't even see or hear her leave. I can't move staring down at this little bundle in my arms.

I've delivered more babies than I can count in my time as a firefighter and a paramedic. This child in my arms right now.....

I freeze in shock when her haunted eyes lock onto me. She looks straight at me from inches away. She definitely sees me.

I can't tear my gaze away. I don't even notice the crew standing around staring at me in abject shock.

Looking at this child does something to me. I don't even know what it is.

She's absolutely, pricelessly gorgeous. She's only a few days old and she hasn't lost the crumpled look of a baby that has just been born.

She moves her tiny hands around in a never-ending symphony of different fingers moving in different directions. Every part of her is impossibly small, adorable, and immaculately precious.

"Chief?" Billy half-whispers in my ear. "What do you want to do with her?"

I drag my awareness back to the present, but I have to summon every ounce of my willpower to take my eyes off the baby.

Just holding her like this changes my body at the cellular level. I dreamed of this moment so many times. Part of me never fully believed it would actually happen.

She doesn't take her eyes off me. She stares up at me with the same rapt fascination that I'm looking down at her.

What does she see when she looks at me? Does she think I'm her father?

Her father. Those words twist in my guts.

I would give anything to feel that for a little newborn baby like this. I would move Heaven and Earth to protect her and give her everything she needs for the rest of her life.

I would be one of those fathers who drives off her boyfriends with a shotgun. I would hunt down anyone who hurt her or even looked at her wrong.

I clear my throat with difficulty and barely glance around the driveway. "Put the hoses away. Secure the truck for our next call. I gotta go upstairs and call CPS."

Chapter 27: Duke

I stumble upstairs to my office thinking fast. I have to report a surrendered child to CPS. I hate to think what they'll do with her.

I get back to my office and try to balance the baby in one arm while I take my phone out of my pocket. I have to navigate on the computer to find the right phone number to call.

I can't call the regular child abuse reporting hotline. The Fire Department has a special social work division we're supposed to call for cases like this.

The baby senses that I'm not holding onto her as securely as before. She also must notice that I'm not making eye contact with her the way I did a minute ago.

She squalls and then starts fussing.

"Okay, okay!" I tell her. "Take it easy. I'm going to take care of you. Settle down."

I lift her onto my shoulder, support her with one hand, and start patting her back with the other. I have to balance her so I don't drop her. I can't work the computer like this.

I use my left hand to hold her in place so I can move the mouse, but she blares off again the minute I stop patting her.

My heart threatens to explode out of my chest. I can't stand the sound of her crying in my ear.

I go back to patting her and she settles down. I don't dare to stop again. I bounce up and down from my knees to jostle her. She seems to like that and the patting.

My mind goes into a tailspin trying to figure out how to keep her calm and quiet. I have no way of knowing how long it will take CPS to send someone out to pick her up—and I haven't even made the call yet.

I'll need to take care of this child in the meantime—which means I'll need to feed her, change her, and help her get to sleep.

I'm just thinking I might go completely out of my mind when Keith walks into my office. I left the door open, so he just waltzes right in. I've never been more relieved to see anyone.

He scowls at me trying to handle the baby and do my job at the same time. "You okay?" he asks.

I barely gasp out, "Yeah! I just....I'm not used to this...."

He gives me another hard, scrutinizing look. "You seem to be doing just fine."

I feel my cheeks turning bright red. The guy has a new baby at home. He knows the drill.

"I got Mandy's license plate number," he tells me. "You might want to give that to the social worker when they come out."

I nod. "Thanks, man."

He bends over my desk and scribbles the number on my desktop jotter pad. Then he straightens up and watches me.

He can see that I have both hands full. I'm not making the call.

"Do you want some help there, man?" he asks.

I start to say, "Could you please....?"

Right then, the firehouse alarm goes off. He looks up at the ceiling and then back at me.

"I won't be able to come out with you this time...." I tell him.

He raises both hands. "I'll handle it. You hold the fort here."

He walks out. Thank the stars in Heaven he's here.

The trucks blast out of the garage with their sirens wailing. The noise of the alarm disturbs the baby. She starts squalling again.

I lift her off my shoulder and move her down into my arms again just as she stuffs her fist into her mouth. Maybe she's hungry.

I scramble to think of a solution. We don't have any baby formula in any of our supplies.

My first thought is to call Leila to help me out, but she won't have baby formula, either. She breastfeeds.

I'm just deciding how I can hold this child in one arm while I phone an Uber to bring me some baby formula when I remember.

Howe Firehouse is a FEMA Emergency Response Center. The firehouse has a reinforced bunker under the foundation and a metric crap-ton of supplies down there so we can respond to every kind of disaster known to humankind.

I hustle down the stairs and have to balance the baby with one arm while I get out my keys to unlock the building understory. How in the name of all that's holy do mothers do all this? I will never understand it.

I break into the supplies. I eventually have to put the baby down while I attack the containers and tear out a canister of baby formula. Fortunately for my sanity, I remember to take a bunch of bottles, diapers, and baby wipes while I'm there.

I don't even bother to take everything back upstairs—not yet. I measure the formula into a bottle, run the water in the sink tap until it warms up, and prepare a bottle for the baby right then and there.

I cradle her in my arm, put the bottle in her mouth, and we both go back to staring deep into each other's eyes while she sucks the formula down.

This is it. This is the moment the last years of my life have been bringing me toward. I knew being a father was right for me. Now I feel it in my bones.

Overpowering love breaks my heart in half when I look into her eyes. I want her. I never want to put her down. I want her right here against my chest for the rest of forever.

I take a minute to sit down on one of the crates of supplies and just let myself feel this. It will all be over as soon as I call CPS. I need to feel this before someone takes her away from me. I'll probably never even see her again after today.

The minute the social worker takes this baby away from me, I'm going to go straight home and do it with Naomi again. I have to hurry up and have my own children—children no one will ever take away from me.

Then I'll be able to pour out all my love and protective care on them. I'll make sure nothing like this ever happens to them.

I'll be able to look down into their eyes for as long as I want and feel this unbreakable bond between us.

The baby sucks for a while, but pretty soon, her eyes start to drift closed. She's falling asleep.

I take that opportunity to go back upstairs. I have to hold onto the bottle, but in a little while, she falls into such a deep sleep that I can take the bottle out and set it aside.

Now I can hold her in one arm while I carry all the supplies back up to my office, relock the building understory, and make my phone call to CPS.

Things go much more smoothly after that—as long as the baby stays asleep. I can carry her in one arm and use my other hand to do things.

I rinse out the bottle and clean the nipple, collect a bunch of blankets from the firehouse laundry stores, and check with dispatch to make sure everything is going smoothly on the call.

It's the case of a lost child on the other side of town. The Police are already initiating a search and the crew is helping out. It's nothing dangerous, and in a few minutes, they find the kid at a neighbor's house.

Police Chief Jim Walker sends the fire crew away. They're just loading up to return to the firehouse when the baby wakes up.

She wakes up groggy and I put her back on my shoulder. I pat her, bounce her, and walk her around my office talking to her the whole time while I try unsuccessfully to do something productive on my phone.

I head over to my desk to put the phone down when an almighty explosion goes off inside the baby's diaper. The concussion reverberates through me with unbelievable power.

I groan and roll my eyes. "Did you actually have to?" I tease and laugh to myself.

She doesn't take the joke. We're going to have to work on that.

I lay out one of the clean blankets on the desk, lay her on her back, and make silly faces at her, and tell her jokes while I start to take her clothes off.

She stares up at me in amazement. She doesn't understand my sense of humor, but at least I'm distracting myself from the fact that I'm about to see her naked for the first time.

I laugh as much at my own reaction as I do at anything I'm doing or saying. Being around this tiny girl makes me giddy and stupid.

She's wearing three layers of body suits, which is way too much for this time of year. Maybe Mandy was so desperate to take care of her baby that she went overboard.

Liquid excrement covers the inside of the innermost layer, but the other two are still clean.

I take everything off, wipe the baby down, wrap up the dirty diaper, throw it in the bathroom sanitary disposal unit, and let the baby lie there on my desk stark naked kicking her feet in the air while she dries off.

I play with her little toes and tickle her under her chin. I'm much more delighted with her than she is with me.

I'm just taping the new diaper around her when the crew comes back and I hear footsteps on the stairs. I expect it to be Keith coming to check on me. I really need an experienced father supervising me on this job.

A middle-aged black lady in a shoulder-length bob wig and a bright dayglo green business suit walks into my office instead.

She takes one look at me putting on the baby's diaper and flops into the nearest chair by my desk. "How you doing, Chief?" she tells me. "I'm Florence Agnew. I'm the social worker assigned to the Fire Department. I was on very familiar terms with your predecessor."

"I'm sorry to hear that," I reply. "Or...I mean....I hope we can be on familiar terms, too."

"So?" She shoots the baby a critical glance while I slide one of the clean body suits over the baby's feet. "A surrendered baby, huh?"

"The mother dropped her off earlier. She said she couldn't do this and drove off. Her name is Mandy and we got her license plate number."

Florence makes a face. "These cases never end well. Once a mother surrenders a baby, she doesn't usually take them back—and she has to go through the courts to get permission to take the baby back even if she wants to take it back. Most of the time, the courts don't grant permission. A woman has to be in a pretty bad place to go that far."

"What are you going to do, then?" I button up the baby's clothes and lift her onto my shoulder. "We can't keep her here."

"She'll go into the system." Florence starts rummaging in her enormous jewel-encrusted purse. "We'll have to find an emergency placement for her. Just don't ask me where we'll put her. Everyone on our books is already at full capacity. I guess I'll take her to the hospital in the meantime."

I gape at her in shock. "Don't do that! You can't just throw her into the foster system! Isn't there any other solution?"

She shrugs that away and barely looks at me. "Not really. The system is already tapped out to the breaking point. We just have to make the best of what we have." She pulls out a pen and a notepad. "What's the mother's license plate number?"

I feel my arms tightening around the baby while I read out the number. Florence jots it down and stashes her pen and notepad in her purse.

She doesn't seem in too big a hurry to take this baby off my hands. A prickle runs up my spine as the moment comes closer when Florence decides to take the baby away from me.

Florence stands up. I would have to be blind not to see how reluctant she is even to touch this baby.

"I'll keep her," I blurt out. "You can emergency place her with me. You don't have to take her to the hospital."

Florence raises her eyebrows. "Are you sure?" She glances around and looks down at the desk where I was just changing the baby's diaper. "You aren't exactly set up for this, are you?"

I don't know how good a job I did, but the baby seems content, now that she's clean. I pat her in a rhythmic motion that keeps her calm.

"I'll work it out," I tell Florence. "I want to. Don't take her. I'll keep her. I'll take her home and give her everything she needs."

She compresses her lips. "All right. It's better than any other solution we have at the moment—but we'll have to do an evaluation on you and your living situation to make sure you pass our criteria as a caregiver."

"Of course!" I exclaim. "That would be great."

She eyes me and takes a minute to say, "You know....once you do get approved as an emergency caregiver, it isn't that much more difficult to get approved for permanent placement. Just something to think about." She turns away. "I have a car seat in my car. I'll bring it up to you ."

She walks out of the office with those words ringing in my ears. Permanent placement.

If Mandy doesn't take this child back, the baby could get permanently placed with me.

My mind immediately switches to Naomi. I have to tell her about this. I have to take this baby to Naomi.

Chapter 28:
Naomi

I open a box on the top of my stack of other boxes, look inside, and sigh. I really don't want to go through the trouble of unpacking these boxes, especially if I'm only going to move again.

Duke is right. We really need to have a frank, fearless discussion—about everything. We need to talk finances, houses, living arrangements—everything. I don't even know if he owns a house in Howe.

I don't know whether he would want me to move into his house or if he wants to move in here—or what.

One thing I do know. I have way too much stuff. I've been living in this house for a long time. I seem to accumulate stuff I don't need.

I put together a different box and start collecting things I don't need anymore. I'll either give this stuff away or sell it.

I'm just going through the bookshelves in my living room when a vehicle pulls into the driveway.

I glance out there and freeze when I see Duke parking his pickup outside. It's still way too early for him to be finished with work.

He gets out of the driver's door wearing his uniform. He must have just come from the firehouse. I sure hope nothing happened.

I stare through the window in absolute shock when he walks around to the passenger door, opens it, and lifts out a tiny baby wrapped in a blanket.

My heart twists when I see him cradle the little bundle in his arms. He looks right down into the baby's face, smiles, and then widens his eyes in an exaggerated clown face.

I stagger out onto the porch as he approaches the house.

I can't even speak when he climbs up and stops in front of me. His eyes shine with so much emotion mixed with sadness, longing, and pure radiant joy.

His voice shakes when he husks under his breath, "I brought you something better than a candy bar."

"What the....?" My eyes dart to the baby.

The little one stares up at Duke in obvious adoration. The baby doesn't take its eyes off Duke once. The little one doesn't even notice me

.

"This is Mandy's baby," he tells me. "She surrendered the baby to me a little while ago at the firehouse. Mandy was trying to find you. We think she wanted to surrender the baby to you, but you weren't there, so I wound up taking care of her."

I can't stop staring at the baby. She's as beautiful, as captivating, and as unbelievably perfect now as the minute she was born.

My knees almost buckle when Duke lays her in my arms. The baby's eyes shift over to me and she stares up at me in the same mindless adoration.

A crushing wave of painful happiness comes over me when I look down into her angelic face. She isn't as rumpled now as she was when she first came out. She's even more beautiful and hypnotic.

"You better take her inside," Duke murmurs in my ear.

He holds the door open for me to stumble into the living room. I sink onto the couch. I can't think. I can't do anything but stare at this heavenly child.

Duke walks away to his truck and comes back with a duffel bag. He unpacks it on the coffee table and lays out a canister of formula, a bunch of baby bottles, baby wipes, diapers, and a stack of clean blankets with, *Howe County Fire Department,* printed on them.

I barely notice, but my world becomes complete when he sits down next to me and puts his arm around me.

"She's magical!" I whisper. "Look at her little fingers! She's perfect!"

"I just had a meeting with the CPS social worker," he tells me. "I got the baby placed with me for emergency foster care. We have to go through the approval process—and then she said we could get approved for permanent placement—if you want to."

My head shoots up and I stare at him. "You mean—we could keep her?! Like—forever?!"

He smiles at me. His eyes overflow with love and emotion. "Yeah," he chokes. "Forever."

"We have to!" I blurt out. "We have to keep her!"

He bursts into a smile and tears come to his eyes. "I thought you would say that. The case has to go through the courts. CPS has to contact Mandy to find out if she wants the baby back—and then the courts have to approve it either way. The social worker wasn't very hopeful about Mandy taking her back."

I turn back to gaze down at the baby. "We're keeping her—as long as it lasts. She's angelic! She deserves the best."

He hugs me around the shoulders and kisses the side of my head. "You better come up with a name for her, then."

I search the baby's eyes for some clue. Who is she? Naming a person for the rest of their life is a big responsibility.

"What about Amelia?" I ask. "That's my mother's name."

Duke looks up and meets my gaze. "Really? That's my mother's name, too."

I burst into a huge smile. "Great! That was easy."

He looks down at the baby and his eyes pour out so much love. "Amelia....Amelia Napolitano....since we're identifying as Italian."

I have to laugh. "Think again, buddy." I look back down at her. "She's so perfect. I can't believe this." My eyes sting and her face blurs in front of me. "She was the one. She was the baby that made me realize I had to quit the Fire Service."

"I know," he murmurs in my ear. "It was meant to be. You two were born to be together."

Duke and I share a long, silent moment of staring down at the baby in my arms. I can't believe this is happening, but at the same time, it does seem to be meant to be.

This baby fixes something that broke when I had to give her back to Mandy.

I feel complete now. I feel like I'm where I need to be and doing what I need to be doing.

Right then, just when I thought my life couldn't get any more blissful, the baby screws up her little face, gives a squalling cry of protest, squirms in my arms, and something like a bomb goes off inside her diaper.

Duke laughs out loud. "I took care of the last one. Now it's your turn."

I make a face. "Thanks a lot. You're so helpful."

He kisses me on the head. "I'm going to make a supply run to the store and then I have to get back to the firehouse. I'm sure you two will be in good hands while I'm away."

"Don't buy any more candy bars while you're out!" I yell after him.

He laughs on his way outside and shuts the door with me and the baby inside alone.

Amelia. Her name is Amelia. I have to start thinking of her as a person because she is one.

She squirms again when she feels her dirty diaper. I have to work fast to clean her up.

I don't want to put her on the floor or on the hard marble coffee table.

I end up spreading one of the firehouse blankets on the couch and lowering the baby onto it.

I move my face close in front of her and talk to her, make silly faces, and make strange noises with my mouth to entertain her while I undress her, but she doesn't respond to anything.

She stares at me and then looks around at nothing.

I can only admire her perfection while I undress her and clean her up. Her little body keeps squirming and twisting in all the wrong ways when I handle her.

She doesn't help me put her arms and legs into her clean suit the way an adult or even an older child would. I have to do everything for her.

I tape up the old diaper and realize I have nowhere to put it. I am going to have to change a lot of things around this house.

I put on her new diaper, redress her in the last clean bodysuit Duke brought me, and wrap a clean blanket around her before I lift her back into my arms.

She fusses when I hold her flat, so I put her on my shoulder. I pat her on the back, sway back and forth, and then pace around the house.

Duke stops by for a few seconds to drop off five grocery bags loaded with supplies—more formula, packs of diapers, bottles, baby wipes, and two big bags of clean baby clothes.

He kisses me once before he leaves to go back to the firehouse.

I hold onto her with one hand while I walk around the house cleaning up with the other hand, but in a little while, she starts squawking again.

"All right. All right," I tell her. "If it isn't going in one end, it's coming out the other, isn't it?"

I laugh at my own joke since I'm not getting any joy from her. I laugh as much at myself as I do at her.

I make her a bottle and sit down on the couch to feed her. We both gaze at each other while she sucks the formula down.

Everything she does is beyond perfect. Every twitch of her facial expression speaks volumes.

She falls asleep in my arms. I don't have the heart to get up and move around. I don't want to disturb her, but I also don't want to disturb myself.

I just want to sit here and bask in the radiant glow of her presence. She's such a blessing. My life will never be the same.

I'm still sitting there when the sun goes down and Duke comes back. He walks in carrying another two grocery bags.

He bursts into a huge smile when he sees me. "I brought Chinese food. I didn't think either of us would be in the mood to cook."

"Thank you," I reply.

"How's the little princess?" he asks.

"Perfect. She's adorable. Do you want to hold her for a while? I've been holding her since you left."

"I would love to."

Chapter 29: Naomi

I ease baby Amelia into Duke's arms and start unpacking the Chinese food he brought home for dinner. I lay everything out on the coffee table and bring over plates and forks to serve everything.

"Would you like me to spoon the food into your mouth for you?" I tease.

He laughs. "I think I can handle it just this once. Thanks. Maybe save it for when our little angel here gets old enough to eat solid food."

I grin back at him and pass him his plate. He holds the baby with one arm and eats with the other.

"We should get her a baby bassinet to sleep in," I remark. "We have nowhere for her to sleep tonight."

"She can sleep with us," he replies.

My head shoots up. "You mean....in the same bed with us? Isn't that dangerous?"

"Nope. My parents slept with me and my two brothers when we were babies. My mom says it's way easier than getting up and settling everybody down multiple times a night."

I blink at him. "I never thought of that."

"It's safe as long as you don't drink, smoke, or do drugs before-hand—and the baby needs to be on a firm surface that isn't too soft—and you can't be too heavy a sleeper. You need to be able to wake up if the baby starts having any kind of distress."

I look back down at her in wonder. "I don't know if I could sleep at all when she's here. I'll just be lying there awake staring at her for the slightest hint that she needs something."

"That's good. You'll get tired enough eventually that you'll have to fall asleep, but that kind of hypervigilance is a good thing. It means you'll pay attention and you won't let anything happen to her."

I look up at him and frown. "How do you know so much about it?"

"My older brother has four kids. He and his wife slept with all of them. I watched them go through it. They were fine."

"Wow," I breathe. "That sounds amazing."

"We can try it as soon as we finish eating. If it doesn't work out or one of us feels that it isn't safe, we can change."

I take another bite of my sweet and sour pork while I think it over.

Duke reads my mind. Considering we've only been doing this for a matter of days, he can pick up my cues like we've been together for decades.

"Is something on your mind?" he asks.

"Since you're here...and I'm here....and Amelia's here....and we're all here....."

He laughs. "Spit it out."

"Now seems like the right time to talk about....well, everything."

"Okay. I'm listening. Where would you like to start? Everything seems like a pretty wide topic, so maybe you could be a little more specific."

"Where do you think we ought to live?" I ask. "Do you own a house in the area? Would you rather live there—or if neither of us wants to move in with the other, we could sell this house and move somewhere completely new."

"I bought a house when I moved to town, but I've only been living there since I started at the firehouse. I'm not attached to the place, so I really don't care if we live there or somewhere else. How do you feel about this place?"

"I'm not particularly attached to this place, either. It's just been a place to live while I spend most of my time at the firehouse. What is your house like? Is it much bigger than this?"

"It's about the same. I have the weekend off from work. We could drive out there and you could take a look at it to see if you like it better."

"What about the baby?"

"What about her?"

"How would we drive there with the baby?"

"The social worker gave me a car seat. We could take her with us. People do it all the time, you know."

I make a face at him. "You mean like....actually drive somewhere?"

"Or we could skip the discussion altogether and just stay here. We seem to be settling in here. I could just sell the other place and we could continue with what we're already starting here. Then you wouldn't have to drive anywhere or go anywhere ever again."

I laugh. "Trying to keep me locked up, are you? I see what you're doing."

He doesn't take the joke. "Now let's continue our discussion from this morning. You said you weren't sure what you would do with your time before we had kids. That question seems to be off the table, now that we have one."

"Yes," I murmur. "It most certainly is off the table."

"Are you happy to stay home with her while I bring in the bacon?"

"Absolutely!" I exclaim. "I wouldn't leave her alone!"

"I didn't mean alone. I mean it seems like a shame for you to give up your medical career."

"No, I want to! This is the whole reason I quit the Fire Service. I'm getting exactly what I want. I can't believe this is all working out so well."

He smiles at me. "You realize what this means, don't you?"

"What does it mean? It means we fast-tracked our whole plan. We've been seeing each other for two whole days and now we have a baby to take care of."

"I mean the part about you getting pregnant. You could get pregnant and you probably will on top of taking care of Amelia. This is going to become your full-time gig."

"I know that!" I exclaim. "That's what I want. Don't you believe me?"

"I just want to make sure we're going in the same direction."

"We are!" I counter. "What part of the way I'm acting tells you otherwise?"

He grins at me. "Nothing. Nothing at all."

He puts down his fork. He's finished eating and so am I. "Do you want some more?" I ask.

"I'm fine. Thank you."

"Do you want something to drink?"

"No, thank you. I just want to sit here and admire this little princess."

He leans back on the couch and gazes down at Amelia's precious face. She shivers in her sleep and settles down again.

I clean up the dirty dishes and pack the leftover food into the fridge. I'm going to have a lot of time during the day to figure out how to feed the three of us in between taking care of her.

Duke is right. I'm going to get as frazzled and sleep-deprived as all the other parents I know.

My life is going to shrink to the most basic survival considerations of sleep, food, keeping the baby clean and dry, and trying to get through the day with my sanity intact.

Tonight is too magical to spend thinking about that. I catch myself smiling at Duke and Amelia—our little family.

They are so beautiful together. I love watching them and seeing how much he loves her.

I can't wait for the years ahead when she grows up and gets attached to her dad. They are going to have such a special bond—maybe even closer than the one he shares with me.

I don't envy either of them that. I love seeing how happy she makes him.

He's going to make her that happy someday. I can't wait to be around to see that.

I fold up the clean blankets, put all of Amelia's dirty clothes and blankets in the laundry, and unpack all the stuff he got for her. I fold up her little clothes and a few more blankets and cleaning cloths.

He's also bought a bunch more bottles, pacifiers, and a few baby toys.

I finally sit back on the couch next to him and gaze down at her, too. I don't want to be anywhere else or do anything else ever again.

"Was there anything else you wanted to talk about?" he finally asks. "We haven't covered everything."

I grin at him. "That's enough for tonight—unless you want to talk about something."

"No," he murmurs down at the baby. "I don't need to talk about anything. I have everything I've ever wanted right here."

I don't try to stop my hand from migrating across the back of the couch. I rub the back of his neck, run my fingers through his hair, and stroke his cheek.

He's beautiful—as beautiful as she is. I really got lucky when I found him.

"Should we try going to bed?" I ask.

"Sure." He starts to stand up and Amelia immediately snaps awake and starts wailing.

"Okay, little sweetheart," Duke murmurs and lifts her onto his shoulder. He kisses the side of her head and starts thumping her on the back, rubbing her, and bouncing her up and down.

He has to scramble to get to his feet and starts pacing up and down with her.

I hover around like an idiot. "Do you want me to do anything?"

"There's nothing to do. She's a newborn baby." He turns back to her and shooshes her into her ear. "Settle down, princess. Everything's all right. Daddy's here. That's right. You're safe. You're alright. You were asleep. That's okay."

I don't know what to do with myself. I want to yank Amelia out of his hands and fix her myself.

Her crying changes when he moves her around. She doesn't stop making noise, but she isn't really crying anymore. She sounds like she's just vocalizing for the sake of making noise.

Chapter 30: Naomi

D uke keeps moving baby Amelia around, pacing back and forth, and talking to her to reassure her.

I flounder in confusion for a minute, but I have to do something.

I go into the bedroom, pull down the covers, and change into my pajamas. I can hear Duke still walking back and forth in the living room. He could be out there for a while.

I pad out there in my bare feet, pick up his duffel bag from work, and rummage through it. I find a few spare uniforms, socks, clean underwear, a plastic container for his lunch, and a stainless steel water bottle.

I take the water bottle and the plastic container into the kitchen, clean them both out, refill the water bottle with clean water for tomorrow, and fill his lunch box with some of my prepared casseroles and other snacks I keep on hand to take for my own lunches.

Or rather I should say I used to keep them on hand to take for my lunches. I won't be going back to the firehouse—ever.

Or maybe I will. Maybe when the kids get old enough and don't need me at home all the time, I'll decide to go back to being a paramedic.

Maybe I should keep my certification current just in case. I don't know. I'll think about that later.

I put the lunch box in the fridge and the water bottle back in the duffel bag.

"Thank you," he tells me when I'm done folding his spare uniforms back in their places.

"You should go by your house and bring your stuff over here."

"I'll do that after work tomorrow."

I wave into the other room. "Why don't I take her for a while and you can change into something you want to wear to bed."

"What would I change into? I don't have anything."

"I have some really baggy, oversized sweatpants. You could try them."

"They would have to be three feet too long for you to fit me."

I laugh at him. "Okay. What would you like to wear to bed?"

"I'll wear my T-shirt and shorts tonight. I'll bring my own pajamas from my house tomorrow."

I wait. "Do you want to come now?"

He follows me into the bedroom, but when he tries to take Amelia off his shoulder, she immediately starts fussing again.

I sit down on the edge of the bed to wait, but he doesn't stop pacing. He just walks and walks and walks—until her diaper explodes again.

He laughs in the baby's ear. "You were building that up for a while, weren't you? Do you feel better now? Come on. Let's get you cleaned up."

I grab one of the blankets and spread it on the bed for him to lay the baby on. He talks to her, jokes around with her, and plays with different parts of her body in between unbuttoning her suit.

He moves her arms and legs around in cheerleading motions, makes her legs bike-pedal, and sings to her while he makes her dance around.

Out of nowhere, she bursts into a massive smile.

"Hey, beautiful!" he chokes. "What a lovely smile you have! You are so gorgeous! Who's Daddy's best girl?"

He bends down and kisses her on the cheek. She gurgles with pleasure and then does it again when he nuzzles into her neck growling like a wolf.

I laugh at them and lay out the clean diaper and wipes for him to clean her up.

He picks her up after he finishes, kisses her, and swings her back and forth while he caresses his lips across her velvety scalp.

"Do you want me to take her for a while so you can get ready for bed?" I ask.

He shoots me a smirk and moves Amelia away from me. "My baby! Mine! You can't have her."

I laugh. "I'm not trying to take her away from you, but you are going to need sleep tonight. You have to work tomorrow."

"So do you."

"You know what I mean. You actually have to function in the world. One of these days, I'll be too sleep-deprived to see straight like you said. Then you can be the one to stay up all night taking care of her while I sleep."

He hands her over and I wrap my arms around her. I hate to admit to myself that I want to keep her to myself. I even want to keep her away from Duke even though I know he loves her as much as I do.

I sit down on the edge of the bed with her while he takes off his uniform. She starts fussing again, so I take her into the kitchen to go through the usual one-handed bottle preparation routine.

By the time I get back to the bedroom, Duke is brushing his teeth in the bathroom. "You better not be using my toothbrush!" I call through the door.

"I'm using mine," he calls back. "You didn't make a very thorough inspection of my duffel bag, did you?"

I sit back down on the edge of the bed to finish feeding Amelia. She's still sucking on the bottle when Duke climbs into bed behind me.

I swing Amelia over to lie her down on the mattress. Then I stretch out next to her.

Duke cuddles in behind me and wraps his arms around me. That should be a suggestive embrace, but I can't stop staring at the baby. Every contraction of her lip muscles is beyond heavenly and perfect.

"Mandy better not try to take her back," I murmur.

"I know what you mean," he breathes in my ear. "I couldn't stand it if anyone tried to take her away from us."

"What will we do if Mandy changes her mind and regains custody?"

He hugs me tighter. "We'll just have to give Amelia as much love as we can while she's with us. We'll just have to do our absolute best for her and hope things play out in our favor. I'll tell you one thing. I won't let her stay with us for a single night without letting her know how much we love her. She's ours no matter what happens in the future."

"Yeah," I breathe. "She is. I love her so much."

He kisses the side of my head. "I love you so much. It might be strange to say that after we've only been together for a few days, but it's true. I can't imagine doing this with anyone else."

I cuddle deeper into his arms. "I love you, too. I love you for giving me this—and I love how much this means to you. I feel so lucky to be here with you—and her."

He burrows deeper into my neck and crushes me in his arms. Then he rests his head against mine and we both go back to gazing at Amelia.

She turns her head to look at us while she drinks her bottle. Her eyes search every detail of our faces.

I just hope she understands how much we love her. I hope she understands, no matter what happens tomorrow or in the years ahead, that she has two parents who would do absolutely anything for her.

I don't know what's going to happen, but Duke is right. I won't let a single day or even a single hour go by without giving her the mother she deserves.

I won't let her live a single hour or a single day on this planet without understanding that she's my daughter, come what may.

Chapter 31: Duke

I scramble around the living room trying to straighten everything that doesn't need to be straightened.

Naomi walks back and forth across the room carrying Amelia around. "Calm down," Naomi tells me. "Everything looks fine."

I wipe my sweaty palms on my pants. "I'm a nervous wreck."

"You're going to be fine. You're the Chief of the Fire Department. You have nothing to worry about."

"What if something goes wrong? What if the social worker finds something wrong with this place—or with us?"

"Just remember what you told me. The foster system is jam-packed already. CPS has nowhere else to put Amelia. They'll be desperate to approve us. Things don't have to be perfect. The social worker just needs to see that we're both responsible adults who are taking good care of her."

I shuffle my feet back and forth trying to fix something that isn't broken. I don't know why I'm so nervous except that I can't stand the thought of CPS taking Amelia away from us.

We've had her for a week and our lives sure have changed.

Naomi and I are definitely feeling the strain of taking care of a newborn. I usually come home to find Naomi frazzled and exhausted after a long day of taking care of the baby.

Then I try to help out and I wind up frazzled and exhausted, too. How in God's name does anyone survive this for years on end?

The thought of anyone taking Amelia away makes me want to kill someone. I really don't trust myself not to go completely postal if the social worker doesn't approve us or if Mandy comes back into the picture.

Amelia is ours, plain and simple. I would defend her with my life. I don't want anyone other than Naomi even touching my daughter.

My daughter. Amelia is my daughter. I don't care what anyone says. She's mine and I'm keeping her.

I still have to get through this interview—and I can't go all Neanderthal on the social worker, either. I have to behave and make it look like I would actually give up Amelia if the State decided that was best.

That is never going to happen, but right then, a car pulls up in the driveway.

I cringe when Florence Agnew gets out. "Oh, no!" I groan. "Not her!"

"What's wrong?" Naomi looks through the front window. "She looks all right."

"That's Florence Agnew. She's the social worker I talked to when Mandy surrendered Amelia. Florence is....."

"She's what? She gave you Amelia, didn't she? She didn't give you any static, did she?"

"No, not at all. I just...." I shift my weight a few more times, but I don't have time to explain why I'm so nervous before Florence walks up to the front porch.

"Open the door," Naomi tells me.

I completely forget to open the door until she tells me to. I pull it open just as Florence is about to ring the doorbell.

I try to smile at her, but it probably comes off as fake. "Hi!" I greet her. "Thank you for coming. Come right in. This is Naomi McFee. She was a paramedic at the Fire Department, but she quit so we could start a family together."

Florence gives Naomi a look and then Florence's eyes dip to the baby in Naomi's hands. Naomi either doesn't notice the look or pretends not to.

She shifts Amelia to her left arm and extends her hand to shake Florence's. "It's a pleasure to meet you. Take a seat. Can we get you anything to drink—or something to eat?"

"No, thank you." Florence sits down all businesslike in a chair across from the couch.

Naomi and I sit down next to each other, but in a second, Amelia starts fussing. Naomi stands up and goes back to pacing.

She and I have developed some kind of sixth sense that tells us exactly what Amelia needs and when.

Amelia likes to move around. She especially likes it when someone walks her around the room.

Both Naomi and I have walked more miles these last few days than in all our previous years alive combined.

Florence doesn't pay any attention either to Naomi's pacing or Amelia's fussing.

Florence takes some paperwork out of her enormous, jeweled handbag, opens a file folder, and she barely looks up at us when she starts marking things off with a pen.

"I see you have a supply of formula, diapers, and spare baby clothes over there on the counter. I'll need to check your sleeping arrangements for the baby and make sure they're safe and adequate...."

"We don't have any sleeping arrangements," I tell her. "We've decided to co-sleep with her."

Florence's head shoots up. "That's extremely unsafe."

"I disagree. My parents did it with three boys and my older brother did it with four children. It's what I'm used to and none of them had any problems. I think if you check the medical literature, you'll find that co-sleeping can actually be beneficial for babies and families as long as it's done with certain precautions—which we are taking. We're both very attentive to ensure that Amelia is taken care of in the best possible way."

Florence raises her eyebrows at me. "Amelia?"

"That's what we named her," Naomi chimes in. "It's my mother's name and Duke's mother's name. It seemed to fit."

Florence purses her lips, bends over her file, and scribbles in it. I'm not sure I want to know what she's writing about us.

"Do you have a primary care physician yet?" she practically snaps.

Naomi and I glance at each other. "Um....not yet," Naomi replies. "We haven't needed one—but I'm a certified paramedic—so technically, we already have a medical professional on hand if something goes wrong....and Duke is a certified paramedic, too."

Florence's eyes shoot back and forth between us. She says, "I see," in the harshest possible tone.

You would think someone who worked for CPS would be the warm and caring type. Don't ask me why they sent out this drill sergeant. They couldn't send someone better equipped to make me nervous.

"Does either of you have any childcare experience in a long-term or professional capacity?" Florence asks still without looking up.

"Um....no....." I reply. "But I used to babysit my nieces and nephews....and I helped take care of my younger brother when I was a kid."

"I helped Amelia's mother give birth," Naomi interjects. "I've taken care of hundreds or maybe thousands of babies and kids during emergency situations. It wasn't long-term care, but it was in a professional capacity....if that counts.....and Duke has done the same thing."

Florence keeps scribbling. She doesn't say or do anything to show if what we're saying means anything.

Naomi shoots me a terrified look, turns away, and hugs Amelia tighter.

"What are your goals, aspirations, and plans for becoming foster caregivers?" Florence demands.

"Um....well....." I stammer. "We would like to get approved as long-term caregivers so we could give Amelia a permanent placement. We would ultimately like to raise her as our own—if the mother doesn't want to take her back."

Florence never stops writing in her file. She doesn't look up at us. "We contacted the mother. She doesn't want the child back. At this point, we're already looking for a permanent placement for the child."

My heart flips. "That's great!" I correct myself and clear my throat. "I mean....it's great for us....and we believe it's the best thing for Amelia, too. We're both committed to giving her the best home and family possible. We believe we'll make the best foster parents for her. In fact, we believe we'll make the best parents for her period."

Florence makes a note of that. I find it hard to believe anyone can treat this process with such cold, clinical indifference. We're talking about a human being's long-term survival and wellbeing, but Florence treats this like some kind of dental appointment.

"What's your marital status?" she asks.

"Um.....excuse me?" I ask.

"Marital status," she repeats. "Married, engaged, domestic partne rship....what?"

I glance over at Naomi. She looks back at me in confusion.

Neither of us answers for so long that Florence actually stops writing to look up.

"We need some evidence of long-term relational commitment," she tells us. "Married is best. Engaged is okay. Anything less than that and we need to start looking at the stability of the domestic living arrangement."

I make up my mind, stand up, and walk over to Naomi. I'm not sure what I'm going to do until I get there, but when I stop in front of her, I notice a loose thread hanging from Amelia's blanket.

I grab the thread, rip it off, and drop down on one knee. I take Naomi's hand and wrap the thread around her ring finger. It's the ring finger of her right hand, which somehow makes it so much more appropriate.

"Naomi McFee, would you please do me the honor of marrying me and spending the rest of your life with me as my wife? I love you and I don't want anything but to live with you forever."

Her eyes well up with tears and her face spasms. "Yes!" she chokes. "I love you so much!"

I kiss her hand and then pull her in to kiss her. Amelia starts squawking the minute I hug them both.

Naomi laughs with tears in her eyes. I go back to the couch and sit down facing Florence. "There. Now we're engaged."

She gives me a look and bends over her file as if nothing ever happened. "I'll need to do my inspection of the premises now." She looks up and casts a critical glance around. "Do you own this house?"

"I do," Naomi replies. "Duke has been living here since we've been together...but he also owns a house across town. We plan to sell it and raise Amelia here."

Florence doesn't seem to hear. She stands up and starts going through the house scrutinizing everything.

I follow her at what I hope is a respectful distance.

She doesn't actually run her hand over surfaces to see if she can pick up any dust. She goes through the kitchen making notes in her files, sticks her head into the laundry room, the bathrooms, and then goes into the bedroom.

Every inch of this house is immaculate. Naomi and I have been working our tails off to clean it to get ready for this interview.

I can't see anything wrong with the house that Florence would disapprove of, but she could probably find something to disapprove of in Buckingham Palace or the Louvre if she really wanted to.

She also goes around and makes a detailed inspection of the front and back yards. I don't go with her this time.

"What do you think she's looking for?" Naomi whispers to me while we wait for Florence to come back.

"I don't have a clue," I whisper back. "I knew she was a battle axe. I just didn't know she would be this bad."

"Now I know why you said, 'Oh, no,' when she pulled in the driveway. She's downright scary."

We go back to watching Florence in silence. We peek at her through the windows while she goes through the yards, bends over to inspect the hose faucets attached to the side of the house, squints her eyes at the fence posts and flowerbeds, and makes a million notes in her file.

She finally comes back to the front porch. I open the door for her to reenter the house.

Neither Naomi nor I make a sound when Florence sits back down in the same place and goes back to scribbling in her file. She better not try to take Amelia away from us on a technicality.

I'm just starting to think about what I'll do to stop her if she tries when Florence asks, "Are you both engaged in full-time employment?"

"I am," I reply. "Naomi has decided to quit her job so she can stay home and take care of Amelia full-time."

"What's your annual salary?" Florence asks without a hint of irony.

"One hundred and fifty thousand," I reply.

Her pen keeps scratching over the page. She never indicates by even a flicker of her eyelash if that's good enough or not.

She keeps writing for so long that I glance over at Naomi again. Her features spasm like she's about to start crying. I might need to call a lawyer after this to appeal Florence's decision....or take some other drastic action.

I really want to go over there and put my arms around both Naomi and Amelia, but right then, Florence snaps, "I'm approving the emergency placement pending the court custody decision. We'll review your case in six months, at which time we'll assess both the living arrangement and the child's medical condition to determine approval for long-term placement."

My heart practically explodes. "Thank you so much!"

She looks up at me, and for the first time, her expression softens when she puts her file folder and pen away. "At this point, I don't see any reason why the custody decision will be anything other than to assign the child to long-term foster care. If the mother doesn't change her mind in the next six months, the child will be placed with you indefinitely. We don't have any other placement for her and we wouldn't likely be able to find a placement as stable as this one anyway. I suggest you get a primary care physician and give the child a complete checkup as soon as possible. Then you can get her another complete checkup right before the interview for permanent placement. The assessing social worker can compare the two checkups and demonstrate that the child is receiving the best possible care and that she's developing well."

"Thank you so much!" I gush. "We definitely will.....and we'll make any corrections you think we need to make to ensure that we do get approved."

She nods toward the backyard. "You might want to remove the nightshade plants from your yard. They're poisonous and young children find those colored berries irresistible. It's one of the leading causes of poisoning in children."

I find myself smiling at her—genuinely this time. "Thank you so much for everything. We will definitely do that."

She doesn't smile back at me, but she casts a much softer look at me, Naomi, and Amelia. "I wish all the placements were like this. She's really lucky to have you."

She walks out of the house. I hustle after her thanking her profusely and babbling like an idiot.

I walk her as far as the porch. She doesn't look back at me when she gets into her car and drives off.

I go back inside to find Naomi shaking like a leaf. "Oh, thank God!" she croaks. "She really had me worried."

I go over there and hug both of them. "We're all right. We're going to be all right. She's ours now."

She huddles in my arms and I kiss her on the forehead. Amelia doesn't like being confined like that, so she starts making noises of protest.

I can't seem to unwrap my arms from around both of them, so I kiss her on the head, too.

"Do you hear that, princess?" I tell her. "You're home. You're safe. No one is ever going to take you away from us ever again."

I let my lips sink onto her soft, precious head. I shut my eyes with a shaky sigh of relief. "I love you so much. We're going to take such good care of you. Nothing bad is ever going to happen to you again. I swear it."

Chapter 32: Naomi

I hold Amelia in my arms while I give her the last bottle of the night. She looks up at me the way she usually does, but her eyelids are already starting to sink.

"I really think she recognizes me now," I murmur. "She seems to be able to focus on me much better. She actually seems to know who it is in front of her."

Duke scoots closer to me from behind, puts his arm around me, and looks down at Amelia's immaculate face. "We're her parents," he breathes. "She must realize that. She sees how much we love her."

"I can't believe I'm actually capable of loving someone this much." I feel myself starting to get choked up. "I couldn't live if someone tried to take her away from me."

"No one is going to take her away from us—not ever." He kisses me on the shoulder. "She's ours and we're hers. We're going to be the best parents on the planet."

"I'll call some of the mothers from the firehouse and find out who they recommend as a primary care physician. I need to make an appointment right away."

"I'll take out that nightshade this weekend," Duke adds.

"I wish I knew what else she put in her file. I wish she would have given us some clue of where and what we could improve on to better our chances."

"After what she said about the doctor appointment and the nightshade, I got the impression that she would have told us if there was anything she was particularly concerned about. She said she wished all the placements were like this. Maybe she didn't write anything bad in her file. Maybe she just had to fill in the blanks to write down exactly what we were doing instead of actually criticizing anything."

"I sure hope you're right," I murmur.

"Don't worry. You heard what she said. Mandy won't change her mind, and even if she does, that doesn't mean the court will give Amelia back to her. We'll get approved for permanent placement and then everything will be fine."

"Yeah," I breathe. "I know. I just wish we could take that element of uncertainty off the table."

"It will happen." He kisses the side of my head. "Six months is nothing."

He settles back on the bed and I do the same thing. Amelia has her eyes closed now. She opens them once when I scoot back on the bed, but she closes them again right away when I lie down and settle her next to me on the bed.

Duke curls in behind me and switches off the light, Amelia keeps sucking on the bottle with her eyes closed.

I watch the movement of her facial muscles. She'll fall asleep now.

Duke buries his face in my hair from behind and I finally let my eyes close. I'm exhausted after our harrowing interview with Florence Agnew.

I want to crush Amelia into my body so no one can ever separate me from her again. I don't want to live without this little person right next to me for the rest of my life. I don't think I could live without her.

I'm just starting to drift off when Duke nuzzles a little lower into the back of my neck. He pulls his hands out from around my waist, squeezes both my shoulders, and then slides both hands down to my waist.

I don't open my eyes, but that touch snaps me back to full alert in a split second. He glides his hands up my sides and squeezes my breasts through my pajama shirt.

I sigh with pleasure. This is the first time we've done anything since Amelia came home to us.

He buries his face and mouth in my neck and crawls up to my ear. His body strains behind me and he presses his hard package into my ass.

He's only wearing a thin pair of pajama pants between him and me. I feel every throb and vein through the flimsy cotton fabric.

He starts unbuttoning my pajama shirt, pulls it open, and then tugs it over my arms so I'm lying bare-chested on the bed in front of him.

He's already shirtless and his warmth floods me when he puts his arms around me this time.

He plays with my breasts and then pushes me forward so my body bends backward to meet him.

He tugs at my pajama pants, but before he can pull them down to expose my ass, he plunges his fingers inside them, slips between my legs, and his fingers penetrate my wet slit.

I gasp out loud, but I can't make any other sound. Amelia lies asleep right in front of me.

I pant and grimace as he winds me up to an explosive release. Amelia being here somehow makes this so much hotter.

Duke and I have to steal these few brief moments while she sleeps. This is our time together before she wakes up and needs constant care from one or both of us.

Duke pulls my hips back against his bulge. I lean all the way forward. I want him to take me on my knees. I want him to plow into me from behind and get all rough and animalistic.

I love it when he does it that way, but this time, he scoops his other hand up my body to my throat, pulls me back against his chest, and drills his fingers in hard.

I gasp out in ragged breaths as the peaks of climax take me. I release myself into his hands and convulse on his fingers.

He pauses just long enough to pull both our pajamas off before he slides into me. His shaft overwhelms me with so much pleasure that I let out one small moan of tortured ecstasy before I silence myself.

He presses his husky mouth against my ear panting hard as he strokes into me. His breath becomes strained and rasping.

He sounds incredible like this. His iron muscles crush me against his chest and his fingers don't stop teasing my clit until I detonate in brutal orgasms.

We both lie right next to Amelia. She's less than a foot away from both of us.

If she opened her eyes, she would see us, but she doesn't open her eyes. She wouldn't understand even if she did see us. She's just a baby, but doing it like this excites me beyond anything I've ever known.

I want Duke so bad. I want to turn over and ride him all night long. I want him to bend me over and plow me to the stars.

I want to roll onto my back and see him staring down into my eyes and know that he's the man in my life who is giving me all the happiness I could ask for.

We can do all those things anytime, but we won't be able to do them all night long—not the way we did when we first met.

He has to work and I have to be alert enough to take care of Amelia all day long. We have to snatch these few moments here and there. That has to be good enough—and it is good enough. It's better than good enough.

He sinks his teeth into my neck at the moment of completion. His rod spasms and he chokes back a broken groan of pleasure when he releases into me. Then he subsides and his arms soften.

I pull off him and twist around in his arms to face him. I turn my back to Amelia—just for a few moments of blissful dreamy rapture in Duke's arms.

I wrap my arms around his neck and kiss him with all the love in my heart. I stroke his hair and face. I can only see the outline of his forehead and cheekbones in the dim light, but I can see enough to feel how much I love him.

"I love you more than anything," I whisper. "We're going to be so happy together."

"I'll go into town after work tomorrow and buy you a real engagement ring," he murmurs. "Then I'll come home and propose to you the right way."

"You don't have to. What you did was so romantic. I love the ring I already have."

"I want you to have the best. I want you to be my wife."

I can't help but kiss him when he talks like that. We kiss for what seems like a long time, but I already feel fatigue creeping up on both of us. We won't be able to stay awake for much longer.

"When do you want to get married?" I ask.

"Do you have a big family?"

"Yeah, it's pretty big."

"I have a big family, too. They would all be really offended if we got married and didn't invite them."

"That sounds like we would need something really big, fancy, and expensive," I point out.

"That's what I'm saying. I think we should sneak off and have something small in an out-of-the-way location. We won't invite anyone. It will just be you, me, Amelia, and whoever marries us."

"An out-of-the-way location.....you mean like Las Vegas?"

"Hell no!" he murmurs. "I was thinking somewhere like Aspen or Santa Fe—somewhere romantic, but remote and reclusive. Then we can have something big, fancy, and expensive later where we can invite both families and all the firehouse crew. We could set the date for six months from now when we get Amelia's permanent placement. We could celebrate it with our wedding—but we would already be married. See?"

I lean in to kiss him again. "I love it. That sounds wonderful."

"Your family won't be offended if we did it this way?"

"I'll explain it to them. My dad and my brothers will probably all want to meet you beforehand, but they can come and visit us here and meet Amelia at the same time."

"That sounds nice," he murmurs. "I'd like my family to come up and visit, too. That sounds perfect."

I kiss him again, but I already sense him falling asleep. He's tired and he has to get plenty of sleep for work tomorrow.

I kiss him once more on the lips and then kiss his eyes, cheeks, and forehead. He doesn't respond anymore.

God, I love him! I can't wait to marry him. He's such a loving father and he already acts like such a loving husband. He's the perfect match for me to build this life with.

I kiss him on the cheek one last time and twist around the other way to spoon into his arms. His arms already feel extra heavy as he drifts off.

He pulls me in against his body, sinks his face into my hair, and doesn't move again. His breathing lengthens.

Lying here naked in front of Amelia with Duke's arms around me floods me with so much passionate desire for him. He's naked now, too.

My body feels round and sexual. My breasts want to nurse a baby and my body wants to get pregnant from his seed. All those sensations, fantasies, and memories wash through me with a tide of desire that almost makes me orgasm again.

Excitement for my future combines with sexual excitement. The pleasure, joy, and fulfillment of being with both of these two people that I love so much—it's more pleasurable than sex. The euphoria expands beyond anything I've ever known—and now it's going to happen.

I'll get pregnant. Duke and I will have children of our own. Amelia will be our oldest and she'll have a bunch of younger siblings running around.

I'll spend my days nursing them, changing their diapers, playing with them, driving them to their after-school activities, and wrangling all their doctor appointments and little emergencies.

I'll probably get annoyed, exasperated, and harassed to the end of my rope just like all other parents do. I'll probably be tearing my hair out by the handful and thinking my life is over.

Right now, I can't think of any greater bliss than going through all that. It sounds like paradise.

Chapter 33: Naomi

A strange sound snaps me out of a sound sleep. It sounds like a loud pop just inches from my head.

I raise my head and my eyes immediately lock on Amelia. Forgotten instinct tells me something is very wrong.

She isn't breathing correctly. She makes a choking noise.

My hand flies to her little body inside her suit, but I already know the truth before I even see her clearly.

My hand darts up to her face and neck. I plan to check her pulse, but as soon as I touch her face, I feel something fuzzy buzzing around there. It sticks to her face and a bee buzzes its wings against my hand when I put my hand down on top of the insect.

I swat the bee away and it falls still buzzing onto the carpet.

"Duke!" I yell. "Turn on the light."

He barely moves in his sleep. "Huh!"

I don't have time to reason with him. I dive across him and crush him under my weight when I switch on the light.

My movements and the light turning on wake him up the rest of the way. "What's going on?" he mutters. "Hey! What are you doing?"

"Amelia's in trouble!" I flip back over to check on her. She's still choking and gasping for air.

The bee's stinger sticks to her face. Her whole head and most of her neck are already starting to swell up from the sting. She gulps her mouth open, but I can already see the flesh inside swelling so thick that she can't breathe.

She can't open her eyes anymore, either. Her neck is way too thick.

I flick the stinger away, now that I can actually see it, but it's too late.

"She's having an allergic reaction!" I exclaim. "She got stung by a bee! We need to clear her airway before she suffocates."

He sits up in bed, takes one look at her, and jumps to his feet. "Get your clothes on! We're taking her to the hospital!"

"There's no time! We have to bring down the swelling now!"

"How?" he asks. "We don't have anything here! We need an ambulance."

"We don't have time for that!" I bellow. "She only has a few minutes or maybe seconds to live!"

I scramble out of bed and charge across the room to my closet. I tear a bunch of crap out of the closet, throw it on the floor, and pull out a zipped nylon case.

"What are you doing?" he asks.

"This is my emergency medical kit. I keep it for emergencies. I've never had to use it, but I have epi in here."

I race back over to the bed. I have to steady my shaking hands while I unzip the case, grab a syringe, and screw on an intramuscular needle small enough for a baby her age.

I snatch the ampule of epinephrine and load the syringe as fast as I can. I try not to hear that Amelia isn't breathing at all now.

Duke sits on the bed next to her and rests his big hand on her chest. "Hold on, princess," he murmurs. "We got you. You're gonna be okay. I promise."

I grab her by the leg and inject the syringe into her thigh through her suit. It has an immediate effect and she gasps in one huge lungful of air.

I give her another injection and then scramble through my kit. "I'm going to give her a shot of Chlorphenamine to bring down the swelling even more."

I give her that one, too. The swelling goes down enough for her to open her eyes and then she starts full-volume crying.

"Oh, precious angel!" Duke picks her up, hugs her, and kisses her ear. "You're all right! Oh, it is so good to hear your voice."

I sink back on my ankles. I'm shaking like a leaf. "We have to take her to the hospital just in case." I look up at him. He's comforting her and bouncing on the bed. Her crying is already starting to go down.

I stumble around the room putting my clothes on. It's one o'clock in the morning.

I take her from Duke while he gets dressed. I put Amelia on the bed and give her a thorough medical exam.

She's still swollen and puffy around the eyes, face, and neck, but she's breathing, crying, and making eye contact the way she should be.

Duke escorts me out to the truck. I zip up my emergency medical kit and take it with me just in case.

I buckle Amelia into her car seat and then I turn all the way around in my seat so I can keep an eye on her all the way to the hospital. I listen with every nerve alert to every breath going into and out of her lungs.

We walk into the Emergency Department and run straight into Ellen Foreman.

She bursts into a huge smile when she sees us with Amelia. "I heard about this little bundle of joy." Her smile evaporates when she sees Amelia's swelling. "What's going on?"

"She got stung by a bee in the middle of the night," I tell her. "She had a really bad allergic reaction. I gave her two shots of epi and one of chlorphenamine already, but she's still puffy."

"She looks like she's profusing well." Ellen takes her stethoscope off her neck, puts the earpieces in her ears, and slips the diaphragm inside Amelia's body suit.

"She has good breath sounds," Ellen decides. "Bring her over here and let's take a look."

She leads me to a nearby exam table, but as soon as I put Amelia down, she starts fussing and crying again.

I pick her up, put her on my shoulder, and bounce her around. Ellen only smiles at me and goes on with her examination while I hold the baby.

"We'll give her a few doses of muscle relaxants and antihistamines, but she should be fine now." Ellen beams at me. "You saved her life."

I don't reply. What else would I do? I'm Amelia's mother. Of course I saved her life.

Ellen and the other medics and nurses keep working around us. They give Amelia the injections she needs and she starts crying again, but her voice sounds so good now.

We stay in the hospital for the rest of the night while the medical team keeps her under observation. The swelling goes down the rest of the way.

Duke goes home and comes back with a bottle for her. She completely passes out.

Ellen won't stop smiling at the three of us. "You can take her home now. Try to get some sleep."

"Oh, I will," I tell her. "I'm not doing anything but the bare minimum today."

Ellen looks up at Duke. "Maybe you should take the day off work, too."

"Maybe I should, but I probably won't," he replies. "Someone has to keep all those rascally firefighters in line."

She laughs and hugs me. "You did great. You should restock your kit in case anything like this ever happens again."

"I will. Thank you for everything."

I carry Amelia outside. The sun is already coming up.

Duke drives us home and I go straight to the bedroom. I put Amelia down on the bed while I change into my pajamas.

He takes a shower. By the time he comes into the bedroom wearing his uniform, I'm already lying down under the covers. I keep my kit within arm's reach.

He kisses me on the forehead. "I'll bring you some more epi and chlorphenamine from the firehouse.....and I'll come and check on you at lunchtime."

I put my arms around him and kiss him. "I love you. Have a good day."

"You, too. Rest up. Don't try to do too much."

He bends down one more time to hug me and kiss me, but right then, I get an overpowering surge of unstoppable nausea. I can't hold it down.

I tear away from him, dive out of bed, and barely manage to stagger into the bathroom before I puke my guts out into the toilet.

Duke comes in behind me and rubs my back. "Hey! What's going on?" he murmurs. "Did you eat something bad?"

I'm puking too badly to answer. The waves keep coming even after I've completely emptied my stomach. Racking spasms twist my whole body into knots.

Duke stands next to me rubbing my back and pulling my hair out of the way. He should leave for work, but he doesn't.

I finally stand up panting and shaking. I pull off a piece of toilet paper to wipe my mouth and then rinse my mouth out at the sink. I gulp down a mouthful of water before I stagger back to bed and collapse groaning.

Duke sits down next to me on the mattress. Amelia sleeps through it all, thank goodness.

Duke rubs my arm and strokes my head. His brow furrows in concern. "Do we need to take you back to the hospital for food poisoning? I feel okay and we've been eating the same food—or maybe you have a virus."

"It isn't food poisoning and I don't have a virus," I croak. "I'm pregnant."

End of Book 7.

Keep Reading

Firehouse Blues Series: Book 8: New Hire

The brave firefighters and paramedics of Howe County Firefighters are pulling together and rebuilding their lives after the disastrous death of Fire Chief John Brewer. New Fire Chief Duke Broebeck is stepping in to fill John's shoes and hiring new people as others leave the service.

Allison Metcalfe fits right into this hornet's nest of interpersonal tension and explosive drama. Her lively sense of humor and friendly, outgoing nature makes her a perfect fit for the closely knit crew.

Firefighter Caleb Watts thinks so, too. In fact, Caleb develops an instant attraction for Allison and becomes convinced that she's a perfect fit for him, too.

There's just one problem. She's already engaged to a doctor from Howe County Hospital and her fiancé is not happy about Caleb paying Allison so much attention. When the two men come to blows, the resulting clash could plunge Howe Firehouse back into a disaster from which it might never recover.

You can find it at your favorite book retailer.

Get All of AE Moran's Free Books

S ign Up Once—Get all A.E. Moran's free books including brand new releases

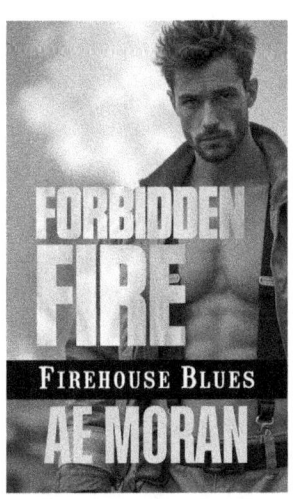

When what you want most is the one thing you can never have......

Austin McAuliffe is every woman's dream firefighter—young, strong, drop-dead hot, and selflessly dedicated to his career—and to the woman of his heart, Emma Brady. Only one other person holds a place in Austin's life—his best friend and fellow firefighter, Theo Gough. Austin insists on Theo spending time with Austin and Emma as a couple, especially when these two firefighters have a hard day at the office.

No one can believe when Austin completely flips out and randomly accuses Theo and Emma of flirting with each other in front of the whole fire crew. Could there be some deeper, more sinister reason for Austin to suddenly lose his mind and lash out at those closest to him?

Emma is devastated when Austin coldly dumps her with no warning and disappears out of her life, but Austin casts a long shadow. The nightmare of his sudden betrayal will come back to haunt Emma and Theo long after Austin is gone. Will the ghosts of the past ruin any chance for them to regain their happiness.....or will Austin's madness take down everyone he cares about along with him?

Sign up at www.authoraemoran.com to read it for free.

About AE Moran

A.E Moran is the contemporary romance pen name for Theo Mann.

I write 70 books per year—and yes, before you ask, all these books are my original creative work. Nothing written under my name is AI-generated or ghostwritten because I write better than AI and any ghostwriter out there.

People don't read fiction for entertainment or to escape from reality. People read fiction to see their humanity reflected in another person's character and story.

This is my promise to you. When you read my books, you'll see your own humanity reflected in the characters and stories. I take this commitment to my readers very seriously. My books are an intimate form of communication between us. I would never disrespect my readers by turning that over to a machine or another writer. This is my bond between me and you as my reader.

I write 20,000 words per day as my daily work output. If anyone with a public platform would like to challenge me to prove this in a controlled environment, feel free to contact me on this website's contact page.

I worked as a professional ghostwriter for fifteen years. Now I'm going for the Guinness World Record by writing 700 books over the next ten years and 1400 books over the next twenty years, all originally written by me. See my website for the full book list.

I'm also the author of *Proof for the Existence of God* and the *Crimes Against Fiction* blog. You can find all my nonfiction work at www.crimes-against-fiction.com.

If you have a story idea, or if you would like me to explore a series in more depth, or if you'd like me to explore a character by writing a spinoff series about that character or world, leave me a message on my website's contact page. I answer all reader emails, so ask me anything, tell me what you liked and didn't like, and let me know where you'd like your favorite series to go. I would love to hear your ideas and find out what you'd like to read next.

You can find out more at www.theomann.com or at www.authoraemoran.com.

Also by AE Moran (so far)